★ "Through Maxine's point of view, readers will become enveloped in the world of skating, cheering her on in competition, in life, and in opposition to the infuriating Alex. They will also find Maxine's predicaments very familiar, as Maxine decides to keep the bullying to herself instead of confiding in her parents. Shen does an excellent job of depicting what racist bullying is like, how it can escalate, and the way it begins to take over every part of a victim's life."
—*Booklist*, **starred review**

"Set in the dazzling world of competitive figure skating, this is a heartwarming story of perseverance and self-acceptance."
—*The Horn Book*

the Comeback

the Comeback

E. L. SHEN

Introduction by Mirai Nagasu

SQUARE
FISH

Farrar Straus Giroux • New York

SQUARE
FISH

An imprint of Macmillan Publishing Group, LLC
120 Broadway, New York, NY 10271 · mackids.com

Square Fish and the Square Fish logo are trademarks of Macmillan and are used by Farrar
Straus Giroux under license from Macmillan.

Our books may be purchased in bulk for promotional, educational, or business use. Please
contact your local bookseller or the Macmillan Corporate and Premium Sales Department
at (800) 221-7945 ext. 5442 or by email at MacmillanSpecialMarkets@macmillan.com.

The Library of Congress has cataloged the hardcover edition as follows:

Names: Shen, E. L., author.
Title: The comeback / E.L. Shen.
Description: First edition. | New York : Farrar Straus Giroux Books
    for Young Readers, 2021. | Audience: Ages 8-12. | Audience: Grades
    4-6. | Summary: Twelve-year-old Maxine Chen dreams of being a
    figure skating champion, but a remarkably talented new girl at the
    arena and a racist classmate at school test her resolve.
Identifiers: LCCN 2020009861 | ISBN 9780374313791 (hardcover)
Subjects: CYAC: Ice skating—Fiction. | Racism—Fiction. | Asian
    Americans—Fiction. | Family life—New York (State)—Lake
    Placid—Fiction. | Middle schools—Fiction. | Schools—Fiction. |
    Lake Placid (N.Y.)—Fiction.
Classification: LCC PZ7.1.S51425 Com 2021 | DDC [Fic]—dc23
LC record available at https://lccn.loc.gov/2020009861

Originally published in the United States by Farrar Straus Giroux
First Square Fish edition, 2022
Book designed by Cassie Gonzales
Square Fish logo designed by Filomena Tuosto
Printed in the United States of America by Lakeside Book Company, Harrisonburg, Virginia.

ISBN 978-1-250-82052-5 (paperback)
10 9 8 7 6 5 4 3 2 1

For my family—my greatest champions.

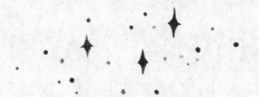

Introduction

Mirai Nagasu

This story, in many ways, captures my childhood. Back then, skating was my future, my dream, and my escape. From the age of five, I prioritized skating over everything, which meant my schedule was full of activities, like ballet, that were meant to help me qualify for national championships. I guess it worked, since that's what happened. But much like Maxine, I considered ballet a medicine that I knew was good for me even though it didn't always taste good.

In third grade, I was placed in ESL, English as a second language, because I used to be unbearably shy and wasn't very vocal. Similar to Maxine, math was not my strongest subject, and language arts became one of my favorites. Like her, I am proud to be Asian American, although I don't recall ever having a talk about it with my parents like she does, where they explain their pride for their cultural roots. It was so refreshing to be able to read about it in Maxine's story.

This story not only captures the microaggressions that many Asian Americans face in the US, but also, importantly, the pressures young skaters face in competition. Whether it is the unending cycle of jumps and other moves we're expected to execute under terrific stress or the fact that we're expected to be beautiful while performing on ice with burning leg muscles and knives on our feet, it can become overwhelming. As competitors, we're taught that there is no room for vulnerability, so it is inspiring to read about Maxine's struggle to be both a great competitor and a great friend.

At one point in the story, Maxine says she considers me one of her role models. This is so surreal. It's also a huge coincidence, because if I had been able to read this book as a young person, I know that Maxine would have been a role model for me.

Like she might be for you.

the Comeback

Mornings

Girls who skate always think they're the next Olympians: *If I just nail that Axel and tweak that three-turn, I'll win gold. I'll become a star. I'll be on TV. I'll make America proud.* You have to be fifteen to be eligible for the Olympics. I've got three more years to go. But I don't just think I'll get there. I promise I will.

"Maxine Chen! Arms up!"

Coach Judy only uses my full name when she's annoyed at me. Pulling me out of my 6:00 a.m. daydreams, she points at my twiggy arms, which have lowered to my sides as I skate around the rink. *An eagle*, she always reminds me, *that's what you should look like.* I grin, wildly flapping my arms as I drift across the ice. Judy rolls her eyes.

Morning curves through the thin line of windows tracing the rink's walls. Outside, shopkeepers on Main Street will soon unlock their doors, offering tourists refrigerator magnets and hooded Adirondack sweatshirts. Kayakers will take out their boats for a final paddle before the lake freezes over. The mountains will stretch from the shadows and graze the horizon. Life will begin. But for now, I only hear the skid of my skates as they power down the ice. This is my favorite form of silence. This is where the magic happens.

I flap my eagle wings all the way to Judy, who is simultaneously scowling and chugging a thermos of black coffee. She may be the greatest skating coach in all of Lake Placid, but she is the worst morning person.

"I can fly higher than an eaaaaagle," I sing to her. "Oh, you are the wind beneath my wiiiiiiiiiiiiings."

I end my serenade with a toe pick in the ice, arms out, head thrown back. I close my eyes for dramatic effect.

"I think this is how I should end my free skate."

Even though I can't see her, I can tell she's smirking at me.

"If you start cawing, I will take you off the ice," she says.

I swing my head back to her, flipping my ponytail over my shoulder.

"Why, Coach, I would never."

Judy sets down her thermos and shakes her head.

"You're ridiculous," she tells me, but a hint of a smile appears on her lips. "Now let's see that double Axel."

I groan. The double Axel is my worst jump. It's the only one where you have to take off facing forward. Then you pull your whole weight into the air and rotate around not once, but *two and a half times*, until somehow you manage to land on your right foot, arms out, left leg extended, triumphant. Honestly, I don't see why figure skaters aren't considered superheroes.

I take a deep breath and start my backward crossovers. I know without looking that Judy is practically boring holes into my skates, waiting for them to push off. I envision her face as nine middle-age judges squinting at me, glasses sliding down their noses, parkas zipped up to their necks, writing down scores that could make or break my entire skating career.

You got this, I tell myself. I imagine Mirai Nagasu before me—she's one of my favorite skaters, partly because we're both Asian American. But what makes her really special is that she's the first American woman to land a triple Axel at the Olympics (that's *three and a half* rotations in the air, which lends her true superhero status). I think of her fist pumped in the sky as she finished her flawless routine, her coach jumping up and down by the boards, the crowd screaming, the tears on her face as she finally delivered.

I push off.

My body feels heavy in the air.

And then it feels like nothing at all, like I'm on one of those teacups from Magic Island Park that's just turning and turning until it comes to a rest.

Before I know it, I'm back on the ice, arms out, leg perfectly stretched. I slow to a stop and look up at Judy.

She's beaming.

"If you do exactly that at regionals," she says, "you'll definitely medal."

It's my turn to pump my fist in the air. I may not be Mirai Nagasu yet, but just you wait.

Self-Portrait

Victoria is mad at me again. I know because she's peering around the side of my open locker door, a massive pout plastered on her face.

"You've got lip gloss on your chin," I tell her.

She sniffs, rubbing at her skin and streaking her finger with sticky pink.

"And you never answered my text," she accuses. Her eyes narrow.

I crouch to stuff my skate bag into my locker.

"No." I shake my head. "I didn't get a text."

Victoria's messages are hard to miss. She put her name in my phone with five heart emojis, six dancing ladies, and three snowflakes so that my notifications explode with a confetti of color. We've been friends since we were eight, mostly because our moms work at the same pharmacy and thought we'd have fun building castles in the makeshift sandpit by the lake. Now, though, she's busy with drama club and softball while I'm permanently stuck on the ice until my thighs burn and my hands are numb. The sand dunes from our childhood have long washed away.

Victoria jabs my shoulder. "You did," she says. "Go look."

"Fine."

I dig out my phone from the bottom of my backpack. Sure enough, buried under four texts from my mom (*How was practice? Do you have enough lunch money? What time should I pick you up from the rink? Hello??*) is a note from Victoria alongside a bajillion smiley faces: *Come over after school 2morrow?*

My shoulders droop. "Ugh, Vic, I'm sorry I didn't see this."

"Whatever," she says. She adjusts her headband

and sniffs. "It's fine. Can you come, though? My sister bought me face masks for my birthday that we can try."

I want to. I really do. But regionals are only three and a half weeks away. I need to head straight to the rink once the final bell rings. Luckily, it's right next to school, so Mom and Dad let me walk there by myself (although they *insist* on picking me up after practice because I'm not allowed to walk home in the dark). That's the beauty of living in a place that prides itself on being a former Olympic Village. The multi-acre arena isn't just the center of my world—it's the center of our entire town. The huge stone building is flanked with international flags and pressed green grass. It symbolizes the excellence of our facilities and our athletes. All the more pressure to nail my routines.

"I can't," I finally say. I look down, fumbling with my backpack strap. "I have practice."

Victoria groans. "Practice, practice, blah, blah, blah."

She takes her hand and forms a talking mouth that almost jabs me in the eyeballs. I can't help but laugh, dodging her fingernails before slamming my locker shut to face her.

My jaw hangs open. Victoria, who usually sports flat-ironed hair and fashion-forward turtlenecks, looks like a giant blueberry. Her sweatshirt bubbles over her thighs and curls around her hands. On one side of the chest is the school mascot, a dragon. Embroidered in white cursive on the other is the name *Macreesy*.

"What are you *wearing*?"

"Oh, this?"

Victoria smirks, holding out her arms like she's modeling for a fashion show and not for the role of Violet from *Willy Wonka & the Chocolate Factory*.

"It's Alex's," she tells me, her voice coated with glee.

I shake my head. "Why are you wearing Alex Macreesy's sweatshirt?"

She shrugs, tossing her hair over her shoulder. "I was cold at lunch, so I took it."

"And you never gave it back?"

She winks at me. "Of course not, silly."

Gross. So this is a thing now? Alex isn't exactly my favorite person in the world. Not only is he annoying in that way most boys are annoying, but he can also be kind of mean. Like the time he picked on a shy new girl for having a smelly lunch. Sure, he's got side-swept hair and sort of muscular arms if you squint really hard, but those things don't necessarily make him parade-around-in-his-sweatshirt material.

The bell rings, and Victoria and I shuffle to art class. Our sneakers squeak on the tile as we weave through throngs of sixth graders. Victoria starts jabbering about all the drama in Drama Club (there's *a lot*), so I replay my double Axel from this morning in my head—my body as it swung through the air, the satisfying crunch of my blade when it hit the ice. I've already nailed my triple toe, so if I can land my double Axel cleanly sixteen more times, I'll be sitting alongside the best of the best in the intermediate division. I can just see myself on the top of the podium, technical elements blown out of the park, biting into that gold medal. Mom cheering, teary eyed as usual, Dad waving his Jurassic video camera in my face. Even Judy will be proud. I close my eyes. The victory almost tastes real.

Victoria grabs my hand, jolting me from my fantasy as she drags me down the hall. Her pale, freckled skin contrasts against my tan wrists. Everyone at school looks like Victoria—ponytails bouncing against the napes of their ivory necks, blushes that turn their pasty cheeks bright red, light eyelashes on bright eyes. I'm the only one here who looks like, well, *me*. I don't think about it too much, but sometimes, just the colors of our hands force me to remember. Mirror Lake may be blue, but our town is as white as the frost layering our windows during the first cold snap.

We reach the end of the hallway and Victoria swings open the door to the art room. I breathe in dried paint and sawdust and let the familiar air envelop me. I love art almost as much as I love skating, although I'm not nearly as good at it. When I do get into a rhythm, though, sometimes brushstrokes feel like crossovers on ice.

I grab a smock from the utility closet, squeeze into my seat, and admire the blank canvas resting on the easel before me. I'm antsy to start as the rest of the students settle in, but Mrs. Bettany takes her sweet time writing *Self-Portrait* on the blackboard. Then she spends fifteen minutes talking about technique and shading, and acrylic versus watercolor. By the time she's done, half the class is smooshing their paintbrushes into their canvases and the other half somehow already has paint all over their smocks. Mrs. Bettany takes a slow, deep breath like she's trying not to scream.

"Okay," she says, "you can begin."

Victoria squeals next to me, rolling up her blueberry sleeves. She dips her brush into purple paint and creates a diagonal line slicing her canvas in half. I wrinkle my nose.

"We're supposed to be painting ourselves, Victoria," I whisper.

Victoria grins. "I *am* painting myself. It's called postmodernism."

"A what now?"

Victoria waves her hand at me. "Never mind." She paints a yellow line across the purple one, forming an X.

I have no idea what she's talking about, so I stick with the basics, mixing white and brown to form my skin tone, followed by straight black hair and pink lips. I paint a little half circle for my nose instead of full-on nostrils, mostly because I suck at drawing noses and want to avoid accidentally making myself look like a pig.

I start on the eyes. As I paint, the wind blows through the branches of a maple outside, its leaves rustling against the windows, orange and red with pockets of green still left from the summer warmth. This time of year makes everything feel like it's changing. Fall marks the beginning of skating competitions. This year, I know I'll be on the podium. My pulse quickens with excitement.

That's when I hear Alex Macreesy's loud breath behind me. I turn, paintbrush hovering in the air.

At first, I think he's here for Victoria, who is literally flinging her paintbrush in his face. But no, he's staring at me, head cocked as he examines my portrait.

"Hi, Maxeeeeeeeeeeeeen," he says.

I try to ignore him and turn back to my painting.

"Hi."

Alex steps closer so that his shirt is almost touching my shoulder.

"I think there's something wrong with your painting," he tells me.

"No, there isn't." I scan my portrait. It's no masterpiece, but it isn't terrible: a long, oval face, two happy eyes, hair draping the shoulders. I even dotted a couple of specks on my cheeks to represent my freckles. Mrs. Bettany would call that *strong attention to detail*.

"Alex, come look at my self-portrait," Victoria calls from beside me, but he's still standing over my shoulder, his mouth widening into a smile.

"Yeah, you made your eyes too big," he says. "They should be narrower."

I freeze. Finally, I can't help but turn my face toward his. Alex lifts his hands, pulling at his own eyes, making them thin and slanted. Then he laughs, bumping my shoulder as he walks away.

My heart plummets. My paintbrush clatters back into the palette, now coated in a muddy brown. Victoria is giggling beside me, but she stops when she sees my face. She shifts in her seat.

"He's just joking, Maxine."

"Yeah," I say, but I can barely croak out the word.

I keep my head to the ground, staring at my sneakers. My face is hot and tears puddle at the corners of my eyes. My thin, stupid eyes. My self-portrait stares back at me, the smirk I so proudly painted now mocking.

Keep it together, Maxine, I tell myself.

Victoria gets up to show off her portrait to Mrs. Bettany, swinging the canvas this way and that like she doesn't have a care in the world.

I take a deep breath and try to conjure the image of Michelle Kwan—one of my favorite skaters—and her perfect spiral across the ice, her face aglow. I focus on her huge smile, her body the only movement on the rink, her gliding blades the only things that matter. *It's fine*, I chant. *It's fine, it's fine, it's fine.* I try so hard to focus on Michelle, but her image keeps flickering in my head. Instead, she's replaced by Alex's laughter echoing in my ears, over and over again.

Wounds

My skates feel like boulders and I'm pretty sure my ankles are blistering. After my tenth failed triple toe, I skid to the boards, kicking up flurries of snow in my wake. Judy is behind me, the big band number for my short program still blasting from her portable speaker.

She raises her eyebrows, a look I like to call "Maxine you are irritating me with that attitude so stop now." The more raised her eyebrows, the more attitude I am apparently giving. Today, her eyebrows are practically lifting off her face.

I know she's going to say that her other skaters, Sam and Fleur, are still on the ice, dutifully running through their step sequences until their parents call them home for dinner. Then she'll tell me that I have twenty-five minutes still left in my practice session, so I better get my butt back out there, lest I waste my parents' hard-earned money. And she's right—that's the worst part.

Up ahead, I can see Mom on the bleachers in her fleece, my gloves clutched in her fists. I hate wearing gloves on the ice, but she always brings them just in case I change my mind. Even from this far away, she looks worried. I sigh and pound my head against the boards. Judy places her hands on my shoulders.

"Maxine, c'mon," she says slowly. "No matter how many times you fall, you've got to get up."

I snort. "Wow, Coach, you're really laying on the cheese tonight."

She spins me around so I'm facing her. The percussion now belts from the speaker tucked under her arm. This is the part where I should be showing off all my footwork, selling my pizzazz and flapper flamboyance to the crowd. Instead, I zip up my jacket all the way to my chin and try to bury my face in it.

"You were doing so well this morning," Judy says. "What's going on?"

"Nothing."

"Well, that's a lie."

It sure is, but I'm not going to tell Judy about Alex Mac-greasy-face. As much as I try to block him out, his pink, gaping smirk still swirls in my mind— the way his fingers stretched the corners of his eyes into taut slits pinging back and forth against the backs of my own eyelids. I try to erase the images, but they linger.

I look up at Judy and say nothing. She shakes her head before releasing her hands from my shoulders.

"All right," she relents, "go home and get some rest. I'll see you tomorrow morning."

She clicks off the music just as it bubbles over, a triumphant finish.

Now it is just me standing pitifully by myself. Judy calls out to Fleur to redo her camel spin.

I unlatch the gate. Mom is already halfway down the bleachers, rushing toward me. Her black hair bobs up and down against her coat, the crinkles in her forehead more pronounced than ever.

"Maxine—"

"Don't worry about it," I say.

She follows me into the locker room, arms crossed.

"What happened? You never get off the ice this early."

I plop onto the bench, untangling my laces and ripping my skates from my feet.

"Nothing," I say. "I'm just tired."

I look down at the red stain seeping through my tights. Great. My ankles *are* bleeding. I yank off my tights, crumpling them into my bag. Like the walking first aid kit she is, Mom instantaneously whips out Band-Aids and gauze from her purse.

"Thanks," I mumble.

I bandage my torn skin and gently wrap gauze around both ankles. I can tell Mom is waiting for me to finish so she can give me a lecture. I won't give her the chance. I move straight from my ankles to my skates, snatching one from the floor and wiping it dry. That's when I catch my reflection in the blade. My dark irises, my eyelids that fold over so you can't see the crease. I blink. What would they look like if they were wider, fuller, with long spider-like lashes—the kind that Alex wouldn't notice? The kind that Victoria wouldn't giggle at?

I blink again and continue rubbing off the melted ice.

Mom inches closer.

"Maybe this is too much right now."

She begins pacing, tangling the leftover gauze between her fingers. "With all your schoolwork and regionals and middle school . . . maybe you don't need to compete right this second."

My head bolts upward, ponytail swinging against my neck. "Of course I need to compete! I have to!"

"Okay, okay, never mind." She collapses onto the bench, her hands up in surrender.

We sit in silence. To make her stop thinking ridiculous thoughts, I almost blurt out everything: the painting, Alex, Victoria's laughter, the way I fell five million times on the ice because his stupid face was stuck in my head. But if I tell her, she'll go do something horrible like talk to the principal. Everyone knows everyone in this town. If Mom so much as lifts a finger, I'll be front-page news for the rest of my life. I want to be a famous skater, not a famous *tattletale*.

Mom crouches down before me, setting her purse on the ground.

"It's fine," I say. "I'm fine."

"You don't *seem* fine."

Her voice comes out in a whisper. She eyes my far-too-forceful blade wiping.

"I think they're dry by now, honey."

I glare at her. But I can't help but notice the softness in her face, the way she tries to smooth out the lines in her forehead to hide her worry.

I remember the first time Mom and Dad showed

me a video of Kristi Yamaguchi in her glittery red dress at the 1992 World Figure Skating Championships. To me, she seemed to float on ice, and the judges agreed—we were all transfixed by her giant smile when she learned that she'd won. Her black, frizzy hair looked like my own. The sparkle in her eyes matched mine, even though I was only six years old. I immediately told Mom and Dad I wanted to be just like her. They didn't hesitate. They didn't laugh at my strange obsession or my seemingly impossible dreams. After all, Dad once had some of his own. He originally moved here to ski. Now he lets me forge my own path.

They took me to the rink and enrolled me in Learn to Skate classes. They sat on bleachers so cold, their legs became numb. Mom hot-glued gems onto my red velvet dress for my first competition just so I could look exactly like Kristi. They don't ever talk about it, but I know that they both take extra weekend shifts as pharmacists at the local Walgreens to pay for my lessons and costumes.

I'm old enough to know that skating doesn't fund itself.

I drop my feet to the ground.

"I really am just tired," I tell her. "I'm sorry."

Mom taps my chin, our secret love pat, before gently tucking a loose strand of hair behind my ear.

"*Shuǐ dī shí chuān*," she says.

I smile, but a balloon of shame fills my chest. I can't help but imagine what joke Alex would make if he heard these words—which lilts in Mom's voice he would mimic, which he would laugh at. But he is not here. I try to remember this. Instead I think about what the words mean. I barely know any Mandarin, but this is the one ancient phrase ingrained in me since I was little:

If you're persistent, you can overcome anything.

Nightmares

I am being chased. Faceless figures in black cloaks follow me down empty, forested roads into seemingly never-ending night. Then the street turns to ice, but I'm still in my sneakers, slipping and sliding and tumbling down a very large hill—no, a mountain. Of course, the creepy figures have skates on and are catching up to me as I tumble. I'm scared. But mostly, I'm annoyed. I am going to have *so* many broken bones from this. Then I'm going to miss the entire competition season. If I could face-palm while falling, I would.

I jerk forward, crashing into the dozens of stuffed animals strewn across my bed. My back is coated with sweat. I blink, adjusting to the darkness. This is my pillow, I remind myself. This is my polka-dot comforter. These are my bandaged ankles and my two brown eyes. And then the memory of Alex stretching his own eyes curdles in my mind. He may not be as terrifying as a Dementor, but I still want to punch him. Or duck for cover. I can't decide which.

I take a deep breath. Maybe I just need a distraction. I lie down on my carpet and stare at the speckled white ceiling. Judy says I'm supposed to do twenty crunches every morning and twenty every night to strengthen my core. In skating, your core is one of the most important parts of the body. If it's strong enough, it keeps you centered during spins and launches you into the air during jumps. I used to feel like my body was gravy sloshing around in an empty can any time I tried to do a single crunch. Now I'm more like mashed potatoes. I can do fifteen in a row easy-peasy. It's the last five that give me grief.

Streaks of moonlight from my window illuminate the carpet as I lace my fingers behind my head and yank my body upward once, then twice, until my back lifts off the floor. Two down, eighteen to go. With every crunch, I try to erase Alex from my brain. Seven. Focus on the ceiling. Twelve. Pay attention to your muscles. Fifteen. Think about brushstrokes. Nineteen. Think about not dying on twenty. Twenty. Think about anything. I drop to the floor, panting. For a moment, the room is hazy. My heart bulges against my chest as my lungs fight for air. But as soon as I catch my breath, Alex's face flickers in my head, his laughter coiling through my ears. He's a cockroach crawling through my brain. I cover my face with my hands before reaching for my phone, parting my fingers to scan the white glow. The numbers on my screen read 11:30 p.m. *Way* past my bedtime. I need to be up at 5:00 a.m. to get ready for practice.

I wriggle back under my comforter and scroll through website after website, but nothing helps me fall back asleep. Soon, I find myself on You-Tube, clicking through makeup videos. I'm watching a tutorial on lipstick application when I notice a suggestion in the sidebar. It's a clip of an Asian girl holding up a peace sign, smiling. Underneath the caption reads: *How I got double eyelids without surgery!* My finger hovers over the icon. I press PLAY.

The girl is talking about this special tape. She calls it double eyelid tape. She takes it from the packaging and dangles it in front of the camera. You can barely see what she's holding, even when you examine it. They're clear, crescent-moon-shaped stickers—nearly invisible. There are about sixteen on a sheet. Carefully, she uses tweezers to lift a single piece of tape and place it on her eyelid.

"Apply it right where you want your crease to be," she instructs. "That way, the tape will cause your lid to fold in that exact spot."

With her eyelid closed, she prods the tape with her tweezers to make sure it stays. Then she does the same with the other eye.

When she opens both eyes, it's almost a miracle. Her eyelids are bigger. Her eyes look wider. She blinks, and you can barely tell that the tape is there at all.

She goes on to apply mascara, all while discussing which eyelid tape is the best to buy.

While she's talking, I open Amazon and quickly type in some of the options she's mentioned. There are packs and packs of eyelid tape, and they're all surprisingly cheap. My fingers are shivering with excitement. I touch the flat ridges of my eyelids, the skin that dips like a collapsed canoe. If I get this stuff, they don't have to look like that anymore. And then I won't have to think about Alex again. For once, I am hopeful.

I linger over the BUY button. Auntie Lillian got me an Amazon gift card for Lunar New Year that I still haven't used. The tape is only fourteen dollars. I click ORDER NOW.

The screen flips to cheery green letters on a white background. *Thank you!* it says. *We're processing your order.*

I press my phone to my chest. My order is processing. It's coming soon, and then everything will change. A tiny smile pulls at my lips, and I, at last, drift back to sleep.

New Girl

"And plié!" Winona shouts, clapping her hands to the beat of the accompaniment.

The pianist's fingers dance across the keys. Twelve girls, doubled in the mirrors lining the walls, their arms out, fingers arched, bending gracefully. Well, everyone, that is, except for me.

"Maxine, dear"—Winona grabs the sides of my waist and squeezes, pushing against my rib cage—"remember your posture."

Yeah, "posture," also known as sucking in your breath so hard that you become dizzy. How am I supposed to skate without breathing?

Unsurprisingly, it was Judy who recommended

me for ballet training. She said it would help with my artistry. You can nail all the jumps and spins, but if you're not elegant, you just look like a flying robot. Personally, I think robots are cool. When I was younger, I wanted to be a part of the ROBOlympians, a group of middle and high schoolers that makes three-foot-tall robots and travels to a technology university downstate to show them off. They win medals, too—everyone is decorated for *something* in Lake Placid, home of the 1980 Winter Olympics. But I never got a chance to join. There was just no way I could make both practice and club meetings.

I press a hand against my tender ribs. Well, if I can't join the ROBOlympians, at least I can pretend to *be* one. I'm about to make my argument on why my bad posture is therefore just a modern choice for a fledgling robot, but I pause when I glimpse Winona's pinched face. Her fire-orange bun perched on the crown of her head makes her look like an exasperated bird. I swallow my words in one large gulp.

"Here, watch me," she says.

Winona spreads her arms out in a 90-degree angle and softly bends to the ground.

"See?" she says in her perkiest possible voice. "Not that difficult!"

Winona Carpenter is a world-class liar. But for the sake of artistry, I return her fake smile with one of my own. Then I suck in so tightly that I think I am literally going to become a pancake. Winona stares at my legs. I plié. She clasps her hands, strands of hair waving across her face like party streamers.

"Yes!" she exclaims. "Much better."

Great. Call me Flat Stanley.

I look at the clock. We have twenty more dreadful minutes and then a twisty ride home. Our town is so tiny that my ballet school is in the village next door. The drive here is short, but the winding mountain passes and figure-eight roads make the trek a dangerous maze. To avoid making multiple trips, Dad ends up waiting in the car out in the parking lot with his favorite sports news and talk station on full blast. Every time I head inside for class, he cranks back his seat until he's essentially lying down and promptly falls asleep. He only wakes up when the commentators mention his beloved Buffalo Sabres before passing out again. I don't give a flying hoot about any sport other than skating, and would do almost anything to avoid watching Dad snore for an hour and a half, but this stupid ballet class is really changing my perspective.

As we work our way through third, fourth, and fifth positions, I play a Would You Rather in my head:

• Would you rather do multiplication tables for five hours or go to ballet class?
• Would you rather sit through *If You Are the One* (Mom's favorite Chinese dating game show that makes no sense because it's in Mandarin and looks

like *Jeopardy!* but with romance) or go to ballet class?
• Would you rather dissect a cow's eyeball (an actual thing we had to do in science class the other day) or go to ballet class?
• Would you rather write a sixteen-page essay on why you hate ballet class or go to ballet class?

Spoiler alert: the answer is never ballet class.

We've moved on to piqué turns. Some of these girls are actual ballerinas, so they've transitioned to pointe shoes. I stand entranced as they pirouette, their bodies like spinning tops.

Then I see her. A new girl turns in the center of the room, rotating again and again and again. Her foot is perfectly pointed, her arms curved in a neat half circle before her rib cage. She's so impressive that everyone pauses to watch her. She looks just like a dancer in one of those music boxes, her sheer wrap skirt a current of waves enclosing her body.

Even the pianist is mesmerized. Finally, the girl stops: one leg delicately extended, chin lifted upward as she stares at her reflection. She's not even breaking a sweat.

Winona is practically whooping.

"Brava, my dear, brava!" She swoops toward the girl. "And welcome to our studio! Remind me of your name?"

"Hollie," the dancer says, blushing. "I just moved here from Virginia Beach."

Now that she's no longer just dizzy circles, I get a good look at her face. Bright green eyes, wavy blond hair tied up in a bun, a small smile that screams confidence. She's at least a half foot taller than I am, making her even more intimidating. Who *is* this girl?

I can hear the jealous ballerinas colluding in the corner, tight whispers filling the studio.

Winona taps a finger against her chin. "Have you thought about joining our dance conservatory? You're really quite fantastic."

"Oh no." Hollie shakes her head. "I'm not really a dancer. I'm a skater."

My heart lurches.

"You *are*?" The words leave my lips before I even realize I'm speaking.

Hollie cranes her neck to peer down at me. "Yeah," she says, grinning with a mouthful of braces. "Are you?"

My head nods, but my stomach is doing more pirouettes than all the ballerinas in the room combined. The puzzle pieces of the new girl start clicking together in my head: Who moves from a beach town to icicle city? Skaters, that's who.

Hollie's face brightens. "Wow! My coach and I are here for the rink." She bounces toward me, her skirt flapping up and down. "You guys have an *incredible* arena."

Don't I know it.

"Cool," I say, trying painfully to act as casual as possible. "What level are you?"

"Intermediate," she says. "You?"

I wish I could plié into a puddle.

"Oh," I squeak, "me, too."

"Awesomesauce! I'm sure I'll see you on the ice all the time, then."

I smile through my teeth. "Yup."

"Well, I'm so glad you've made a new friend, Maxine!" Winona interrupts. "But let's get back to work."

The pianist starts up again with a ragtime medley. Winona demonstrates a pas de chat, and we follow suit, a jumble of arms and legs. I watch Hollie, who looks like she was born to dance. I feel like a prancing goat.

All I can do is look up at the mismatched tiles on the studio ceiling and pray to the skating gods. Please, I beg them, please, please, *please* don't let this girl be as good a skater as she is a ballerina. I can already see her on the podium, waving and grinning with her dumb turquoise braces matching her turquoise dress, her posture impeccable.

Then there's me, stooped on the sidelines as Mom tells me there are always more competitions, don't worry, *next time*. I scrunch my nose and stretch out my arms.

Hollie from Virginia is *not* going to ruin this for me.

On Fire

Clearly, the skating gods didn't listen to my prayers. Hollie is not just a good skater, she's flipping *fantastic*. At practice after school on Wednesday, I watch as she zooms down the ice on a forward outside edge and into a double Axel, double loop combination. A double Axel combination jump! And here I thought I was so high and mighty landing one clean double Axel all by its lonesome. I fight the urge to bury my face in my mittens.

Carmen's "Habanera" belts from the overhead loudspeaker. Hollie's coach is tracking her every move, clapping vigorously to the beat as Hollie transitions into a layback spin. We both watch as her head and torso effortlessly lower, like she's simply falling back into pillows and not contorting her body into a practically inhuman position. She could give Sasha Cohen, queen of laybacks, a run for her money.

Hollie's coach apparently thinks otherwise. He's shaking his head, bleached blond hair flapping against his temples.

"Focus!" he barks. "This is baby stuff!"

I flinch from my spot in the corner and hug my elbows. The rink feels colder.

Fleur drifts toward me, a sly smile etched onto her lips.

"His name's Viktor," she whispers. "I think he's Russian."

She skids to a stop and leans close. "I heard he used to coach with Team Turgenev."

Team Turgenev? They're basically the best coaching team in the entire world. They're based in Moscow and run by Sabrina Turgenev, a coach so intense she could melt a skater into a puddle on the ice with one sharp glance. A lot of her skaters quit early because their bodies break under the pressure. But when they push through the pain, they're golden. They're always on top.

I gulp. "So why did he leave?"

Fleur shrugs. "Guess he found something better."

Our eyes slowly turn once more toward Hollie. She's speeding down the rink on a forward outside three-turn. Triple Salchow. I squint. Not even the slightest bit under-rotated.

"Honestly," Fleur says, "she's incredible."

Heat tingles in my fingertips and burns through my cheeks. I want to look away but I can't. Fleur's eyes are wide and glassy, as if she's been hypnotized by a twelve-year-old girl and her slightly terrifying Russian coach. My teeth clench.

"Girls!"

We hop backward as Judy screeches at us from across the rink.

"Get to work!"

She's helping Sam with his sit spins, but he keeps leaning too far to the left and toppling over. Judy's fists are balled in her hair.

Fleur snorts. "Well, at least there's no competition there."

She tucks her braid into her jacket collar and twizzles down the ice, executing tiny, tight spins with style.

I bite my lip and start my backward crossovers. Fleur's words seep into my veins. *No competition there*. I dig my blade deeper and follow Hollie as she zooms past in an elegant spiral.

"Maxine!" Judy calls. "I want to see that triple toe."

Hollie moves from a spiral into a catch-foot. Oh, I'll show her my triple toe. No problem.

I point my arms and three-turn, holding my position until I'm ready to launch. I'm skating faster than ever.

One. Two. Three. I hold my breath.

Takeoff.

I hurl my body into small revolutions. I'm a marionette on a puppeteer's string, winding and winding before the release. And then the string snaps. My toe touches down, blade pressed into the ice, left leg extended. Chin high, I glide.

Judy nods. "Excellent. Great work, Maxine."

I peek over at Hollie, but she's got her body stretched into a vertical split, her eyes straight ahead. Sam stumbles over, his mop of ringlets sloshing into his face.

"Yo, you were on fire, Max!" he hoots, slinging an arm around my shoulder.

Hollie is hunched over, panting against her knees. I lean back into Sam's embrace. Huh. Who's *incredible* now?

Why Math Class Is the Worst

In all six years of elementary school, Alex Macreesy and I managed to avoid having a single class together. Back in the good old days, I blissfully skated down Mirror Lake Middle School's checkered hallways and onto the ice, gliding past the sharp line of his laughter. Now? I cross paths with him in not one but *three* classes a day: art, math, and history.

In math, Ms. Valencia waves a laminated grid in our faces and announces my worst nightmare—a new seating chart. She calls out the assignments one by one.

The smart kids are in the back so they can use algebra as nap time. Victoria is dead center because she'll watch Instagram videos all class unless someone keeps an eye on her. And I'm far right, by the window, so I can thankfully blend into the scenery. Much to Victoria's delight, she's seated behind Alex so she can gaze at the back of his head. But as soon as he starts to sit down, Victoria giggles, a grating tune that refuses to let up through Ms. Valencia's lecture on order of operations. Our math teacher frowns.

"Alex," she says, "on second thought, please move over there."

She points to the desk right next to mine, just three feet away from my quiet corner of sunlight.

"Oookkkay," Alex says, walking over and sliding into his seat.

He seems to have reclaimed his stolen sweatshirt. Admittedly, it makes him look a lot less like a blueberry than it did on Victoria. She crosses her arms, cold and grumpy now that she's all by her lonesome.

I stare straight ahead, my eyes glued to the blackboard. I'm determined not to look at him. Alex taps his pencil against the desk, a steady rhythm growing louder. I focus on the numbers: $8^2 - 3^2 \times 4$. Eight squared. Eight. Squared.

The 8 on the page reminds me of a figure eight, and my mind curves into lines sliding across the ice. Hollie's jumps may be better than mine, but her edges have nothing on my footwork. Despite her unearthly ballet skills, she tilted on a rocker turn this morning, and Viktor was so disappointed, he didn't even yell, just shook his head. My rocker? It's so perfect, I could frame it.

I glance down at my planner peeking out from underneath my math work sheets. October fourth. Only two and a half more weeks until North Atlantic Regionals. Judy and I scoped out the competition last weekend—other than Hollie, it should be the usual faces: Fleur, who's arguably more graceful than any of us but can barely complete a double Lutz, much less a double Axel; Gwen from New Jersey Skating Club, who twisted her ankle and may not even make it to regionals; and Katarina from New York Skating Club, who's a powerhouse but as inconsistent as my math grades this year. I just need to work on fully rotating my double Axel, perfecting my triple toe, and nailing my combination jumps, and I *know* I can medal. You have to finish in at least fourth place to make it to sectionals, so my placement really counts. Panic rises in my chest. I try to focus. Nathan Chen, also known as the quad king (that's *four and a half* revolutions in the air), zips around my brain before skidding to a stop. His curly hair dips between his eyes. He winks. I stifle a smile.

Crack! Alex's pencil splits in half against his desk. The class snickers, and Ms. Valencia sighs, shaking her head.

"Whoops," he mutters.

"Here." Ms. Valencia pulls out a sharpened pencil from the tin on the chalkboard and offers it to Alex.

She walks back to the front of the room, glancing at the clock. "Actually, you'll all need sharpened pencils because I'm giving you a pop quiz."

We all groan. Victoria buries her face in her hands.

"Don't worry," Ms. Valencia assures us as she passes the quizzes down the rows, "it should be easy and will only take about ten minutes. I just want to make sure you know your fractions from last week."

The packet lands on my desk. Multiplying and dividing fractions. Okay, I can do this. After skating practice last Thursday, Dad sat with me in the dining room and went over my fractions homework one question at a time. Thankfully, this might be the only unit this year I fully understand.

I start on the first question, digging my pencil into paper. To my right, sunlight scatters across the page. To my left, Alex's desk seems closer than ever. And then his elbow inches toward mine. I peek out from behind my quiz. Alex's face tilts, his eyes glancing down at my paper as he sniffles. He cranes his neck to get a closer look.

I immediately swing my arm around to cover my quiz.

"Stop," I hiss, keeping my eyes down.

"What?" he whispers innocently.

"You *know* what." I hunch over my desk, my nose practically touching the page as I scribble my answers.

He scooches closer. "Come onnnnn," he says. "I just need a little help."

I finally turn my face toward his, piercing daggers with my eyeballs. His grin only widens.

"But you people are good at math," he whines. "Can't you just be useful?"

My breath hitches. "You. People?"

Heads swing toward us and I can hear heels clacking up the aisle behind me.

"Maxine? Alex?" The sharp twinge in Ms. Valencia's voice bounces off the classroom walls. "Please stop sharing answers."

At once, twenty-four heads turn. Alex hunches in his seat. My neck is sweating and my pencil shakes against the paper.

"No, Ms. Valencia, I wasn't—"

But Ms. Valencia just holds a finger to her lips. She surveys the rows of staring eyes and looks back at me, casting an invisible spotlight over my head. On the ice, I'm struggling to nail a showstopping performance, but here, I'm apparently made for the silver screen.

"All right, everyone, back to work."

She shakes her head just slightly, lips pursed before her skirt swishes away. I don't dare look at Alex, although his forehead is probably pasted to his desk. I grip my pencil to stop my hand from shaking.

Focus, I tell myself, *come on, Maxine.* I picture Mirai Nagasu, muttering silently to herself at the

US Championships, fists clenched before she starts her free program. *I'm not a cheater!* I want to shout. I'm not a cheater and if I were to start, it wouldn't be with Alex Macreesy, the boy whose cackles are just loud enough to get under my skin, who thinks he can tell me all about my slanted eyes and then turn around and steal my answers. Because "my people" are good at math. Well, joke's on him. He should have cheated off Victoria instead.

The clock ticks. Five minutes left. Slowly, I exhale to the image of Kristi Yamaguchi, poised in the center of the ice, unafraid as the music begins. My mind clears inch by inch and I manage to scribble down the last two quiz answers. The bell rings.

In an alternate world, I get up, drag Alex along, and march over to Ms. Valencia. I'm like Nathan Chen, determined to redeem himself after his disastrous short program at the 2018 Olympics. I force Alex to admit that he was trying to cheat off me, that I had nothing to do with this. In an alternate world, Alex cowers sheepishly and Ms. Valencia offers me a profuse apology.

Instead, I sit, frozen. Ms. Valencia collects everyone's quizzes, shuffling papers as students linger to ask about homework assignments and extra credit. Alex scoops up his books and slings his backpack over his shoulder. He half smiles at Victoria, who is waiting for him by the door while pretending not to. She trips over her ballet flats, and stumbles.

I instinctively get up, and we lock eyes as she catches herself on the doorframe. She glances my way, but her eyes glaze over my face. It's like she doesn't even recognize me.

And then both of them are gone, and I'm by myself.

Even Nathan Chen winking doesn't seem that appealing anymore.

The Package

As we pull into the driveway, I can see the small cardboard package sitting on our front doorstep, half hidden by an overgrown shrub. I know immediately what it is. Mom doesn't seem to see it, thankfully. She's still too busy trying to figure out why I haven't said much about my day.

"How was art class?" she asked on the car ride home, studying my face through the rearview mirror.

"Fine."

"Science?"

"Good."

"Skating?"

"Okay."

"Spanish?"

"Bueno."

"Math?"

Nothing. What was I supposed to say? The math teacher embarrassed me in front of the whole class because Alex tried to cheat off me? I apparently now have zero friends in school? I'll pass, thanks. I can just imagine Mom's face if I told her: anxious eyes quickly filling with darts of anger, furrowed eyebrows as she pulls the car over and takes out her phone, using her scary mom voice to ring up the school and demand answers. I'll have to drown myself in Mirror Lake if she does that. The coroner can label my body: *Maxine Chen, death by phone call to principal.*

Mom is about to pull up to the garage when I press a hand to her shoulder.

"Wait!"

She brakes, and we jolt forward in our seats. She turns to me, startled.

"Sorry," I say. "I just thought maybe I could bring up the trash bins tonight."

Mom's face brightens. The empty bins need to be rolled up our driveway and to the garage every Tuesday. I am usually very adept at whining so Mom will do it instead. I mean, the bins are empty, but they're heavy and have that nasty leftover-garbage smell. But today, I am more than willing. If that package is what I *think* it is, then there's no way I want Mom seeing it or questioning me about it. I do my best to fake a wide-toothed smile. Mom looks so pleased I think her head might detach and do a cartwheel around her neck.

"Oh, thank you, Maxine," she says. "That's very mature of you."

I nod a little too vigorously, swinging my backpack over my shoulders and speeding out of the car before she can become suspicious.

The trash bins smell just as putrid as I thought they would. I flip the lids closed and clasp the handles before waving her forward. She cruises up the driveway and into the garage. I roll up the bins *very slowly* so that by the time I reach the garage she's already inside our house. Success.

Now it's time to practice my ninja skills. I take pointers from ballet class and relevé, heels lifted, sneakers tipped off the ground in order to make as little sound as possible. Then I jog across the grass to the front door, ducking under the kitchen window to sneak the package into my backpack, and zip back to the garage. This probably only takes about thirteen seconds. Maybe if skating doesn't work out, I'll become a world-class sprinter.

When I swing open the door to our mudroom, the electric garage door grinding shut behind me, I can see Mom peering into the fridge. She pulls out ground beef, a carton of eggs, scallions, and dumpling wrappers.

"Dad should be home in five," she says. "I thought we could make dumplings tonight."

Dumplings are our favorite collective comfort food. There's something really calming about sitting at the kitchen table together, listening to reggae (Dad's go-to), spooning spiced meat onto paper-thin dough and folding the wrappers so intricately, each dumpling could be a little work of art. Mom's always the best at it. Her dumpling folds could have their own Instagram account.

"Yum," I tell her, gradually backing up until I reach the staircase. "I'm just gonna do some homework upstairs first."

"Mmm," Mom replies, looking down at her phone.

I bounce up the stairs and shut my bedroom door behind me. This is my happy place: medals hooked all over my walls, interrupted only by posters of Michelle and Kristi and the other greats. I plop down on my comforter and slowly unzip my backpack. The package is sandwiched between my take-home folder and math textbook. I can't even think about math, and Alex, and the way my cheeks flamed. I fling the textbook out of my bag, determined to hurl the memory from my brain. And then I move on to the most important thing—the package. Gingerly, I lift it onto my bed and slice open the packing tape with a fingernail.

Most of the package is just pink Bubble Wrap. And then, at the bottom, I spy a tiny plastic container with brown cursive scrawled across the top: *Magic Methods Eyelid Tape*. Through the plastic, I can see the crescent moon stickers, dozens and dozens ready to be peeled and placed on my lids. Just like the YouTube girl said: *Apply it right where you want your crease to be. That way, the tape will cause your lid to fold in that exact spot.* Good-bye, collapsed canoe lids. Hello, big eyes. I finger the package, examining each magical sticker.

"Maxeeeeeeen." Dad's voice floats up the stairway alongside his favorite Bob Marley album. "It's dumpling time!"

He's so dorky, but I can't help but laugh.

"Coming!"

I stuff the tape under my pillow and run downstairs. Mom and Dad have already created an assembly line of ingredients: meat and chives, flour and dumpling wrappers, cascading down the kitchen table. Dad is shoulder shimmying to Bob Marley, which is definitely not the correct way to dance to Bob Marley. Mom tucks my hair behind my ears and throws a Grinch apron over my T-shirt and leggings.

"You don't want to get flour all over your clothes," she says, reaching behind to bunny loop the apron's ties.

We push in our chairs and Dad hands me a wrapper. I spoon a tiny ball of meat into its floury center before dipping my fingers in water and gently rimming the dough. It always seems like it won't work, but water seals the dumplings and keeps their creases in place. To me, it's a small form of wizardry. Dad is already pinching his dumpling shut, although it looks like a puffer fish with meat ballooning from its sides. Mom laughs, rolling her eyes at his lopsided creation.

"So," Dad says, "how was school today, Maxine? And practice?"

"Fine."

Mom sighs. "Apparently, that's her only vocabulary word today"—she dramatically waves her hand in the air—"*fine*."

To be fair, at least practice *was* fine. I landed two double Axels. My Biellmann spin stayed centered on the ice. But I don't want to talk about any of it. As I trace my finger across a second wrapper, Alex's sneer keeps pushing through its center, followed by Ms. Valencia's pursed lips, that slight shake of her head, the way her heels clacked away like a door slamming in my face. I don't think either of us got any points deducted from our quizzes, but that doesn't erase Alex's nasally voice, the "come onnnnn," the "you people," the "can't you just be useful?"

You people. Can't you just be useful? I cup the dumpling in my hand. Mom hums along to *I, I'm willing and able.* She looks so happy. The dough flops against my palm.

"Maxine, honey, you okay?" Dad's voice cuts through Marley's smooth melody.

I look up at Dad's floppy black hair, one strand curled over his forehead, wire-rimmed glasses pushed up on his nose. The uncooked dumplings piling on the plate in the center of the table, Mom twisting dough into origami boats. This is just what Alex Macreesy thinks *we people* do. We are exactly what he pictures when he leans over my desk and copies my answers.

I swallow. "Yeah, Dad, I'm fine."

Nighttime Secrets

The house is quiet. I'm pretty sure Mom and Dad are asleep. Slipping my hand underneath the pillow, I grope blindly for the package of eyelid tape until I find its plastic rim. Just where I left it, thank goodness. I yank at my comforter and hop out of bed, pulling my hair into a high ponytail. Time to prepare for battle. Tape? Check. Scissors? Check. Tweezers stolen from Mom's makeup bag? Definitely check. Peeking through the sliver of light in my doorway, I check for signs of life. The coast is clear.

Once I'm in the bathroom, I flick on the lights

and gently close the door. My skin stretches before me, this time a real blank canvas. One for me to paint as I wish. Under the harsh glow, I can see every freckle and line. The droopy curves of my eyelids. The flat ridge of my nose. Maybe Alex was right—my self-portrait looks nothing like me.

I rip open the package and take out the folded instructions. *Peel away the strip and trim as needed.* I inspect one strip and hold it up to my eye. I try to cut it a tiny bit shorter, but it's so flimsy that I feel like I'm going to ruin it. It looks like sticky paper. I paid fourteen dollars for this? *Shake it off, Maxine,* I scold myself. *This is what you've been waiting for.*

I keep reading. *Identify where you would like your new eyelid fold to be. Place the strip right above the crease you want to create.* I lift the tape onto my skin, but my fingers struggle to stay still and the tape flops all over my lid. It lands in a haphazard, dangling line.

Okay, so I'll start again. It can't be this hard. Finally, I get it in a spot a quarter inch above my crease. Progress. *Press the tweezers into the tape to adhere it firmly against your skin.* I push and push until my eye feels like it is being jammed into its socket. At last, I face my reflection in the mirror.

Everything feels super weird, like my eye is bent in this strange direction that it doesn't like. The worst part is: I look even more awful than I feel. My eyelid is permanently surprised. My face has transformed into a shell-shocked gargoyle. And you can see the tape—it's not invisible at all. It's an off-white, pasty sticker just sitting on my skin.

I blink a couple of times. Maybe the tape just needs to adjust to my eye. But the more I move, the more its edges pinch and peel.

I'm an art project gone wrong.

Wildly, I rip it off. The tape leaves behind a red mark, a raging half-moon that could never conceivably be my eyelid crease. I sink to the tile floor, my handiwork now strewn around me. The bright red mark rests above my barely there monolids, cruel and relentless as it sneers: *To think you could change. What a silly, silly girl.*

Main Street Blues

"What's that on your eye?"

Mom stops Main Street traffic to roll up her sleeves and poke at my eyelid. I swat her hand away.

"Mom, seriously, we're in public!"

"Okay, okay." She raises her palms in surrender.

"I probably just rubbed them too hard when I woke up, that's all," I mutter. It's a bad excuse, but she's no longer paying attention. She's too distracted by Fleur's mom, who's just left Vesper's Bookstore and is furiously waving at us.

"June!" Mom calls, putting on her fake Adult Voice.

June scampers to us in yoga pants, leaves crunching underneath her sneakers. "Beverly, Maxine, how funny running into you here!"

This town is five feet wide, I think. *You literally run into everyone everywhere.* Still, I smile and nod while June chatters endlessly about Fleur's seventh-grade classes, her pet labradoodle, and regionals, of course, which, *can you believe it*, are only a week and a half away. While Mom attempts to make small talk, I stare out at the mountain-dappled skyline. The cobblestone sidewalks are scattered with tourists. By December, they'll be teeming. To live up to its reputation as a winter sports wonderland, Lake Placid always pulls out all the stops with toboggan rides and snowshoeing, warm cider, and twinkle-light shops jingling with ornaments to take back to the city. American flags line the lampposts as if to alert every visitor that we are the pride and joy of United States athletics. I touch the mark on my eye. An all-American town.

"Anyway, I'll see you at the rink later," June

finishes. "Phil's got a hockey game, and then Fleur has practice, so I'll be there all day. Lucky me!" Her hollow laughter echoes in my ears.

Mom touches June's shoulder in a way that seems friendly, but really means *Bye now!*

"Absolutely," she says.

When June is out of sight, Mom shakes her head. "That woman could talk my ear off."

We stop in front of Bob's Skate Shop and swing open the door. It's the only skate shop in town, but it's verifiably the best in New York. I always try to get my skates sharpened ten to twelve days before competitions. I don't want to skate on dull blades, but I also don't want to experience any new sensations during my performance. Everything should feel exactly like I've practiced.

Bob comes out from the back with goggles strapped over his hair. He looks like Dr. Frankenstein.

"My two favorite people!" he exclaims.

"Good morning," Mom says, gently removing the skates from my bag.

He scoops them into his arms like newborn infants, already knowing what I want before I've even asked.

"I'll be back in ten," he says.

Mom smiles. "Such a pro."

Ten minutes is totally enough time for me to start the math homework crumpled in the bottom of my backpack. Mom always makes me bring homework everywhere I go because I never have enough time to do it. But math *is* hard and terrible, so I immediately pretend to be really invested in the new skate guards hanging in rainbow colors down the wall. Mine are boring and black, but these come in shades like "silver spiral" and "layback lilac." My personal favorite is "tangerine tango," a flashy orange that would pair magnificently with a gold medal around my neck.

I dangle my choice in front of Mom's face.

"Can I get these?"

Mom pushes her hair behind her ears and looks down at me with exhausted eyes. She'll never admit it, but she gets just as restless as I do before competitions. I know she wants all my hard work to pay off.

She flips over the tag and looks at the price.

"No, Maxine." She sighs, pacing between the apparel and accessories aisles.

"Pleeease?" I say, knowing I shouldn't.

Mom snaps her head toward mine so quickly, I hop backward.

"Maxine, we've already spent loads on your other stuff."

I pout, following her eyes as they trail down my Patagonia parka; fleece-lined, over-the-boot skating pants; and Zuca figure skating bag waiting patiently by the register for my freshly sharpened skates. My costumes sit in my closet at home, one elegant and black to match my sleek short program, the other light blue with tiny jewels running down the center. As Judy would say—delicate but beautiful.

Dad always reminds me that money doesn't grow on trees, but it's easy to forget when you're clutching tangerine tango skate guards that bend like new rubber. I loosen my grip. I don't even really care about them anyway.

"Sorry," I say. "I know."

Mom ruffles my hair. The whirring stops. Bob reemerges, shiny skates in hand.

"All set, kiddo."

I grab them by the laces, marveling at their metallic shine. Slowly, I run my finger along the edges. A rush of excitement floods my body. I can't wait to get on the ice.

Bob rings us up, and Mom fishes for her wallet in her purse, emerging with her credit card. She slides it across the table.

"Before practice, you're doing your math homework," she says without looking up.

I groan.

"Don't think I didn't notice."

I sling my backpack over my shoulder and roll my skate bag toward the exit.

When I make it to the Olympics one day, I'll earn a bunch of money from endorsements and Stars on Ice and stuff. Then I won't have to do math or school or any of that boring junk. I'll become rich and famous. And I'll pay Mom and Dad back for everything.

Dress
Rehearsal

Five days later, I dangle my arms across the boards
and watch the Zamboni's sharp blades shave off a
thin layer of old ice, leaving a perfectly smooth surface behind. I love being the first to skate across the
clear-as-glass surface—it feels like I can do anything.
As the driver finishes up, I pop off my guards, ready
to skate. Judy holds me back.

"Not yet, Maxine. Hollie's first."

On the sidelines, Hollie dons a cotton candy
dress over her tights and becomes a pink blur as
Viktor counts her jumping jacks. In the days before

a big competition, we each get individual time to rehearse our free programs. Of course *Hollie* gets to go first.

"Fine," I mutter.

Hollie from Virginia bolts onto the smooth ice, ruining it with her blades. She moves into starting position and nods to the audio guy. "My Heart Will Go On" echoes through the rink. Usually, we have to play our music on our own speakers so everyone can hear their programs, but now, with only Hollie on the ice, the *Titanic* anthem croons from the PA system. I crinkle my nose.

"Celine Dion is a little cheesy, don't you think?"

Judy nudges my ribs. "Be nice."

Fine. But just because Hollie is skating, it doesn't mean I have to look. Instead, I throw my leg up on the boards and stretch out my hand to touch my toes. Then I move into spiral position, pointing my foot as far as it can go. I imagine I'm Michelle Kwan performing her signature spiral curving down the ice. I swing my arms back, a smirk toying with the corners of my lips. Who needs Hollie when you're the greatest skater of all time?

Viktor's interrupting screams and rapid hand movements aren't helping, though. Okay, fine, I'm looking.

Hollie ends her skate with a scratch spin before flinging her arms across her chest in a melodramatic embrace. The music cuts off and Viktor cheers so loudly, he might just crack my eardrums.

"Six out of six!" he shouts.

I want to remind him that the judges don't score out of six anymore, but *whatever*.

Hollie skids off the ice and gives me a huge braces-filled smile. This time, her rubber bands are pink. Of course. They match all the loooooove she's emoting on the ice.

"Have a good skate, Maxine," she says as she waltzes past me, Viktor on her heels.

"Yeah, thanks." I fight the urge to roll my eyes.

I do a lap around the rink as Judy yells to keep my arms steady in the air.

Yup. No time for flapping wings now. This is crunch time.

"All right, let's do it." She gives me a thumbs-up as I glide to the center of the ice.

Just give it your all, Maxine.

The opening fluttery piano scale curls through the rink speakers. Gershwin's Concerto in F is my favorite. It's classy and sassy, two things I strive to be as a skater and a person. I first heard it when watching a rerun of Yuna Kim's 2010 Olympic gold medal free skate. She's a Korean skater whose grace and elegance are unparalleled. I can't match her artistry, but maybe through this program, I'll hint to the judges that I can get there someday soon.

A homage to Queen Yuna's subtle cheekiness, I begin my program by blowing a kiss to the air before three-turning into twizzles across the ice. They seem simple, but if you falter just the littlest bit, you could tilt and fall on your butt. This time, though, my twizzles are so clean, I could be an ice dancer.

Maybe it's Hollie's irritatingly good skate etched in my memory or the red welt still imprinted on my eyelid or the newly sharpened line of my skates slicing the ice, but I am fired up and unstoppable. Double Axel? No problem. In fact, I get so much height that I'm practically bungee jumping into the air. Double Salchow, double toe—a breeze. Triple toe—check. I transition from a layback into a Biellmann spin, one of my newest elements. You lift your blade behind your back and then all the way up over your head. Then you somehow spin while holding this position. It seems like an impossible move, one which requires inhuman flexibility. But I've been stretching at the boards twice a day before practice. At home, I clutch my bed frame and arch my back until my head reaches my foot. *Tip as far as you can go*, I tell myself. *Don't be afraid*. And I'm not— I'm fearless. I don't even feel the usual ache in my spine as I turn in ice-carved circles.

I almost forgot how beautiful spinning blades can be, how the wind that I create as I twirl through the rink swirls like magic. Time seems to float by. Double Lutz, double loop. Camel spin. The piano crescendos. Sit spin.

My blade cracks against the ice. Arabesque. Double flip. Now everything melts away: Alex, Ms. Valencia, and Asian eyelid tape. Only my blades, only the rink exist. I end my program with an arm lifted above my head as the music fades to silence. I am weightless.

And also *really* out of breath. I suck in air and search the rink for Judy. That last spin made me so dizzy that the whole world seems to be in motion.

Judy skates over to me from the boards. Her face is all pink, her eyelashes clumped together in wet bunches.

"Coach," I half laugh, half gasp, "are you crying?"

"Be quiet," she says, wiping away tears.

She cups my face with her gloves. "Maxine Chen."

Oh no. My full name, that can't be good.

Judy shakes her head.

"No matter what happens next week, you should know that you're a terrific skater. I'm so proud of you."

My body is doing invisible somersaults.

"Oh man, Coach," I say. "Don't make me cry, too!"

A Revolution

At school on Friday, I bounce to my locker, humming along to Gershwin, still on a high from my all-time best practice. I glance at my reflection in the mirror inside my locker door. In the glass, I catch Alex and Victoria chatting several feet behind me. She's clutching her science binder—the one we decorated together with magazine cut-out letters and YOU GO, GIRL! stickers from her mom's craft drawer.

Alex leans in and whispers in her ear. What on earth could he have to *whisper* to Victoria? Probably something stupid, like "I'm failing math," or "I accidentally dumped an entire bottle of gel in my hair this morning."

Nope. I shake my head. *You've got better things to think about.* Like how I'm going to slay this competition on Saturday. I look back at the mirror, studying the freckles splattered across my cheeks, the red mark on my eyelid now a faded line, practically invisible. I stuffed the eyelid tape in the bottom of my bathroom drawer, and I plan on never letting it see daylight for the rest of eternity.

Still, as I glance at myself in the glass again, I can't help but examine the flat ridges of my skin, the way they curve over my lids so that all you can see are my short eyelashes peeking out. I inhale sharply. *It doesn't matter. It* doesn't *matter.*

I slam my locker shut. Usually Victoria walks with me, but of course, she has other *friends* now. I roll back my shoulders and strut down the hallway. Whenever I'm dragging my heels, Dad always tells me to keep marching. Who needs Victoria when I'm not only capable of marching to class but parading to regionals and kicking butt on the rink?

When I arrive, I slide into my seat and bury my nose in my history textbook, catching up on last night's chapter that I fell asleep reading. When the bell rings and everyone files in, I pretend to not even notice Alex drumming his pencil against his knee in the back of the room.

Our history teacher, Mr. Warren, sits hunched over an egg sandwich, engrossed in some novel. I squint: *Catherine the Great: Portrait of a Woman*. It's always the same routine with him—egg sandwich, thick biography, funky round glasses. The only thing that changes is the color of his spectacles; he loses them so often, he buys a new pair about every other week. Today, they're a mossy green.

"All right, everyone, quiet down!" he says to an already mostly silent classroom. Flecks of egg have settled in his mustache.

He turns to the whiteboard and writes in fat letters: *REVOLUTIONARY WAR*.

Half the class groans. "There are so many *wars*," someone says.

"Yes," Mr. Warren says, "and there are many more to come." He pauses. "Now who can tell me about the Revolutionary War?"

Elisa, a girl with red hair in two high pigtails, shoots up her hand.

"It's when the Americans won their independence from the British."

"Correct!"

Mr. Warren wipes a hand across his eggy mustache and begins writing furiously on the board. I stifle a yawn. We already went over this in fourth grade. This is baby stuff. Thomas Jefferson, the Declaration of Independence, Washington crossing the Delaware, blah, blah, blah. There were the redcoats and the colonists, and stuff about taxation without representation, and a bunch of white guys having a tea party while dressed up in problematic Native American costumes. I remember that Mom volunteered to help me study for the test on this topic, but instead of going over the flash cards I'd made, she kept going on long tangents about power and privilege and the symbolic importance of the Boston rebels dumping tea into the harbor. Honestly, if she weren't a pharmacist, she'd be a great politician.

I peek at the board. Mr. Warren is still scribbling, but I can make out some of the words behind his head.

Crispus Attucks. Henry Knox. Mercy Otis Warren. Moses Brown. Abigail Adams. Roger Sherman. John Paul Jones.

He whirls around, arms crossed against his paisley button-down.

"Now," he says, "who recognizes any of these names?"

Silence. Someone sniffs. I can hear Alex rolling his pencil back and forth against his desk.

I bite my lip. Well, maybe I don't know *everything* about the Revolutionary War.

Mr. Warren smiles triumphantly.

"That's what I thought."

He returns to the whiteboard, underlining names.

"A lot of people know about the big players in the Revolutionary War, but most don't know about the unsung heroes. These are just a few of them."

Mr. Warren walks to his desk drawer, pulling out a fedora. He makes a show of waving it in the air. Mr. Warren is like the Adam Rippon of teaching— ever entertaining, although Adam never has an issue with egg-sandwich shrapnel.

He scoops up a bunch of little pieces of paper from the desktop and drops them into the hat.

"This month, we're going to be putting on skits."

"*Skits?*" Alex cries.

I crane my neck to see Alex groaning from the back of the room, his spit spraying across Elisa's desk.

Elisa gags, rolling down her sleeve and wiping it along her desk's rim.

"Yes, *skits*." Mr. Warren grins. "You're each going to pick a name from this magical hat"—he holds out the fedora like a cauldron—"do some research on your unsung hero, and then write up and perform a short skit for the class from the perspective of your historical figure." He pauses. "I'll give you step-by-step instructions after you choose your figure. We'll be working with Mrs. Lovell, the librarian, on best research practices."

He moves down the rows. Hands fumble in the fedora and emerge with scraps of paper.

"I suggest writing down the names of your unsung heroes on your phones, your planners, your foreheads, whatever," Mr. Warren says. "I know how easy it is for you kids to lose things. And forget things." He winks at Alex. "And I don't want any excuses for missed work."

Following Mr. Warren as he weaves down the aisles, I watch as Alex shrinks down in his chair.

Mr. Warren approaches my seat. "Find your hero, Miss Chen." He smiles.

I dig my hand into the hat and pull out a crumpled paper: *Mary Ludwig Hays*.

I don't know who she is, either. But I guess now is a good time as any to find out.

Ballet Blunder

Mary Ludwig Hays might have to stay in my back pocket for now. Literally—I stuff the slip of paper in my jeans pocket and promptly forget about it for the rest of the day. After all, I have bigger things to worry about, like my twisted ballet skirt refusing to untangle itself in time for class. I fling it around the locker room, whipping it like a kite before giving up and watching it deflate on the ground, still knotted.

"Maxine Chen?" I can hear Winona calling from the studio. "Is she here?"

"Coming!" I yell, yanking the coiled ties one last time. Blessedly, they come undone.

I quickly put on the skirt and dart to the nearest open spot as Winona moves into fifth position. I turn my feet and try to ignore her when she pokes my butt because she wants me to suck in.

"Your glutes, Maxine," she whispers at a volume still loud enough for the entire class to hear.

The ballerinas by the window titter, their lips barely moving so as not to seem indelicate. I sniffle. Maybe they should change career paths and become ventriloquists.

Under the harsh studio lights, the dancers kick up swirls of dust as the pianist drags his fingers across the keys into a Chopin melody. My leotard feels scratchy against my skin and my tights rub against my ankles. I close my eyes and imagine myself in bed, snuggled up in my blankets, a loose corner of my Kristi Yamaguchi poster fluttering in the cool night breeze. If I concentrate really hard, maybe my head can magically transport itself to a soft feather pillow.

"Plié!" Winona's thin screech breaks through my

daydreams. I open my eyes a sliver to see her giant nest of orange hair bobbing in the center of the studio as she pliés against the mirrors. I bet birds could lay eggs in that bun.

The pianist abruptly transitions from Chopin to a musical theater jive. The upbeat melody hurts my ears. I glance around the studio. When Winona's not looking, I purposefully push out my butt into a full-on squat. This is my plié protest. Or, it almost is, until my butt hits the front of a gauzy skirt, and the person attached to the skirt trips backward.

I twist around to see Hollie blinking at me, her mouth forming a tiny, perfect O. My butt is still poking out as she cocks her head at me, a few perfect strands of curls cascading down her cheeks. My face flushes, and I snap back to standing position.

"Sorry," I mutter.

"It's okay, Maxine," she says, pushing back her hair, her forehead crinkled. "But I don't think that's how you—"

"Yes, I know," I bark.

Of course she would use this moment to try to scold me, with her delicately bent knees and graceful fingertips and mocking, sugar-sweet voice.

She blinks. "Okay, sorry."

I scowl into another plié. I can hear Hollie's shoes take a step backward. The pianist is getting hammy with the musical theater medley, his fingers dashing across the keys. My scowl stretches to my chin.

Winona bounces over to me.

"Smile, Maxine." She lightly touches the corners of my mouth. "There are no angry ballerinas in here!"

Now even the pianist is snickering. Have I mentioned that I despise ballet class?

At last, the clock hits seven thirty. I beat the rush to the locker room, pull my sweatshirt over my head, grab my backpack, and jet out of there faster than you can say relevé.

The sun has set and the parking lot is getting darker by the minute. When I get to the car, I have to bang on the window because Dad is, as expected, lying down in the driver's seat with 580 Sports Radio blasting.

"DAD!" I shout.

My fist hits the glass at least five times before he shudders awake and snaps off the radio. Then he fumbles around for the button to unlock the doors.

Two cars down, Hollie and her mom swivel their heads toward me. Even in the dim light, I can tell that they both have the same irritating forehead crinkle. I bet when they drive home in their dumb minivan, they will giggle at the clumsy Chinese girl who butts into people when she pliés.

Dad squints sleepily at me, offering a lazy yawn as he maneuvers his seat back to a sitting position. He finally unlocks the door, and I climb into the car.

"You could wake up a little faster, you know," I mutter.

"Well, hello to you, too."

He makes a show of swinging his head back and

forth to wake himself up. I shake my head. What a weirdo.

We swerve out of the parking lot and onto the spiraling mountain road, the sky blackening.

"How was ballet?"

I curl myself against the window. "Terrible."

Even with my eyes closed, I can sense Dad looking at me.

"Huh."

He pauses. "You know, if this ever gets to be too much for you, with skating and school and ballet and regionals—"

"Dad," I snap.

"Got it, yup, end of conversation."

I lean my head against the window, peeking out at the lonely road, falling asleep to the light hum of the Ford's heater. Right now, I wish I could just stay permanently in this car. Even though I'm theoretically closer to my blankets and my pillow, I still have two Pythagorean theorem worksheets to do and I haven't even begun thinking about Mary Ludwig Hays. Maybe one day, when I join the ROBOlympians, I can build a robot that does my homework for me and then puts the information in my brain while I sleep.

Dad turns on the radio again, flipping through stations until he lands on nineties hits.

I groan and cover my ears. "It's so loud," I whine.

He takes a hand off the wheel to flick my shoulder. "But it's your favorite."

I weakly pop my head up from the window. It's TLC's "Waterfalls."

Sometimes we have to travel really far for competitions just to reach mostly empty rinks with overpriced food and a handful of spectators. I'm better about it now, but I used to get really antsy during car rides, especially if they were several hours long. So Dad began blasting this nineties satellite radio station as a form of distraction. We made it all the way to Jersey and Pennsylvania powered by the Spice Girls, Destiny's Child, Green Day, R.E.M.,

Snoop Dogg, and Sir Mix-a-Lot. When we got *super* bored, we'd make up little dance routines like we were in some early YouTube music video. Even Mom would shimmy in her seat.

Now, Dad crows along with the song.

He winks at me, his head bopping up and down. I lift my head from the window, my mouth unconsciously spreading into a smile. Dad starts doing some strange shoulder roll, and I can't help but laugh.

"Come on, Maxine!"

He is relentless. I toss my bun dramatically and then join in.

"That's the spirit."

The car flies down the road, *Don't go chasing waterfalls* bubbling through our speakers. The ride is short, but the night seems to go on forever. I sing with Dad until the music lulls us home.

Competition Day

"Eat up," Mom says, her hands outstretched.

I stick my nose into the still-steaming bowl, the lotus leaf wrapper puffy and hot. Sticky rice, sweet soy sauce, juicy pockets of egg, and slivers of crispy sausage ooze from the sides of the wrapper. Lo mai gai is my favorite thing to eat the day of a competition. The meat and eggs keep me full and the palm-size portion ensures that I'm not *too* stuffed before my big skate. Mom hands me a pair of chopsticks and I dig in, the sauce instantaneously sliding down my throat and calming my nerves. Still, I can't help but run through every move in my short program, like I'm suddenly going to forget something.

Double Axel, triple toe, I silently chant, *camel spin, sit spin, lunge—*

Dad interrupts my merry-go-round of thoughts, patting my tightly wound bun.

"Wow," he says, "you really sprayed that thing into place."

He studies his hand, now coated in a thin layer of hair spray, before turning to the sink to wash it off. I pat my hair to ensure he didn't ruin my perfect chignon. I probably used about sixty-five bobby pins to keep it in place.

"Well," Mom says, "we don't want any hair snafus while Maxine's on the ice."

I nod in agreement, but my brain is back on the carousel: *double Lutz, double toe, spiral, layback—*

"Max? Did your teachers email you the homework you're going to miss?"

I shift my gaze to find Mom scrolling through

her phone contacts like she's going to dial Mr. Warren and Ms. Valencia any minute now.

"Mom! Yes!" I shout, flailing over the counter so she won't successfully humiliate me forever.

"Ooookay, just checking."

She glances at Dad and rolls her eyes when she thinks I'm not looking. I cross my arms. Because we're one of the youngest groups of girls, we compete on Thursday and Friday and miss two days of school. It means I'll have a bit more homework to do this weekend. So what? That's the least of my problems. I run through my step sequence—wait, it's brackets, then forward twizzles, right? Or is it the other way around? Oh no.

"Ahem."

Mom has put her phone down, and now leans over the granite, eyes bulging at the lo mai gai and then back at me. I roll my eyes and take a big bite. She smiles, satisfied. I know she won't let me leave the house if I don't finish my food. *Food is fuel*, she always tells me, *especially for a skater.*

I swallow. Did Nathan Chen feel this nervous before his back-to-back world championship wins? When you get to that level, does your stomach still do backflips? I bet it does, with all those cameras on you and the world watching on live television, just to see if you'll mess up. At least I'm not under that kind of pressure—not yet.

I fish a chunk of rice and sausage into my chopsticks. Girls who skate always think they're the next Olympians. One day soon, I'm going to get there.

Sing, Sing, Sing

I have never been good at waiting. Even though I've stretched in the locker room and practiced all my jumps on the jigsaw mats, I still can't help feeling like a jittery jelly bean. On deck in my black dress with the deep U curving down my bare back, the velvet rubbing against my sheer sleeves, I chatter in my skates. Judy rubs her gloved hands against my arms. I do a couple of squats to keep myself warm. We stand at the precipice of the rink, in the little side hallway with the peeling walls and rubber floors.

"Remember, home ice," she repeats, a mantra to keep me calm.

One of the perks of living in Winter Olympics Capital (or as Dad likes to call it: "the second Canada") is that most of the big competitions are held here. It's got five indoor rinks inside the arena to offer simultaneous sessions of hockey, synchronized skating, practice, and competitions like these.

Home ice. I know every one of these red bleacher seats, every harsh light beating down, every scratch on the boards' walls. This *should* make me calmer. But instead, everything feels strange: all these girls—not just the intermediate ladies like me, but tiny three-foot skaters caked with blush, and elegant junior teens with flamingo legs and flicked eyeliner—make the rink feel alien. Like it's not mine at all.

They're just about to announce Katarina Novak's short program score. From here, I can see the tiny Kiss and Cry box where Katarina and her coach are probably boring holes into the monitor by their feet that will decide her current fate. The nine judges are dots sitting at tall black tables on the other side of the ice. Regal and stone-faced, they're like the Supreme Court justices of figure skating. At a lower table, three technical specialists carefully replay each element on a slow-motion video.

I inch to the boards, Judy by my side. The booming voice overhead announces Katarina's score and pockets of applause echo from the thousand-capacity rink. There are only forty to fifty people here—families and locals mostly, since tourists only come for national and international competitions. But I don't care. I'm not performing for them. I focus on the merry-go-round: *double Axel, triple toe, camel spin, sit spin—*

"Our next skater is Maxine Chen, representing Lake Placid Skating Club."

Mom and Dad are cheering far too loudly from the bleachers. Even though they sit at the top to avoid distracting me, I know they'll spend the next two minutes and forty seconds holding their breath, clutching a packet of Twizzlers and trying not to look every time I'm about to jump.

"Go get 'em," Judy says.

As I skate onto the ice and rest my hands in starting position, the silence seems to stretch infinitely and horribly. It feels like a year has gone by before the opening drums of "Sing, Sing, Sing" fill the rink. And then the saxophone belches and I'm in motion.

The steady, rising beat fills my ears as I dance down the ice.

Now, my hardest element—the double Axel. I breathe into my backward crossovers, pumping my legs to pick up speed. I flick out my wrists, extend my back leg, three-turn so I am facing forward, and then, finally, push off.

I am floating.

And then I am

really,

really,

not.

My blade slips and my hip hits the ice before I even realize I am no longer in the air. Snow streaks my dress. My tailbone stings with pain.

The chaos of saxophone and cymbals and drums crowds the rink's walls. I can hear gasps in the bleachers.

Keep going, I know Judy is thinking, and I have to. I *have* to. I quickly rise to my feet and continue my program. I try not to think about my body splintering, Mom's hands pressed against her temples, Dad's video camera slowly lowering, Judy's held breath.

Thankfully, I make it through my triple toe without crashing, and I keep a plastic smile on my face through the rest of my elements. I just want this terrible cacophony of drums and saxophone to stop. Just, please, stop.

Camel spin. Sit spin. The merry-go-round goes faster and faster. It refuses to let up. I tilt on my double Lutz, double toe landing. I can already see my technical points sliding down my score sheet, like the snow now melting on my dress. My layback is clunky, not delicate.

But then the drum rhythm accelerates, signaling

the end of the program, and I'm spinning until I can't breathe. Then, thankfully, my toe pick hits the ice. It's over.

I curtsy twice before speeding off the ice. Judy ushers me into the Kiss and Cry, her mouth moving a mile a minute.

"It's just the short program. You completed two rotations in the air before you fell and the judges will count that. Your triple toe was solid, you'll get a high grade of execution for that. You under-rotated your double Lutz, double toe, but you had a clean landing, so you shouldn't receive too many deductions. Your layback wasn't perfect, but I don't think you'll lose points. And your edges were strong. Good job keeping up that smile. Remember that you tried your best, and that's . . ."

Judy's voice trails off as she watches me. I plop down onto the bench and stare glassy-eyed into the monitor.

"It's just the short," she says again, like she's reminding herself, too.

I don't say anything back.

Hollie is last to skate. I can see her glittery red dress from here, her thin fuchsia lips, her curls perfectly pinned to her head. As I watch her sailing past, I have the urge to leap back onto the rink and cross-check her into the wall like a hockey player.

"The scores, please, for Maxine Chen."

I lean forward, my arms gripping my sides.

"For her performance, she has earned a score of 33.01. She is currently in sixth place."

Judy is patting my back.

"Not that bad," she says, her voice squeaky and high-pitched. "It could be worse."

I shake my head.

"Sixth," I manage to choke out. "I need to be at least fourth to make sectionals."

Then I remember Hollie. When she's done, I'll probably be *seventh*. To think I was sure I'd medal. Look at me now.

"Maxine"—Judy's voice lowers—"you have an entire free skate to go."

But I'm not listening to her anymore. I run out of the Kiss and Cry and smack straight into Mom and Dad, who immediately try to wrap their arms around my shoulders.

"Just remember what that famous skater Yogi Berra said," Dad offers. "It's not over till it's over."

I don't even know who that is or what that means. All I can think about is my butt hitting the ice. So I rip myself from their grasp and stomp into the locker room. Alone.

A Tough Landing

The crowd is going wild. Even though I'm curled up in the corner of the locker room, skates still on, I can hear their distant cheers.

"For her performance, she has earned a score of 45.15. She is currently in first place."

Hollie. In first place.

The announcer babbles on about the conclusion of the short program, but I can't listen. The room swirls before me, dizzying and dreadful. Suddenly, the door swings open. There she is, golden curls, sticky lip gloss, a huge braces-filled smile on her face. There are a handful of people in the wings, but I somehow only see her.

Before I can escape, Hollie notices me in the corner. I spring to my feet.

"Good skate," she says. "I'm sure your free will be even—"

"Are you serious?" I blurt. "Just go away."

Hollie's mouth opens, and then closes.

Immediately, I know I've done something terrible. Her face drains of color and tears prick her eyelashes. She stands there, frozen, like she doesn't know where she is, like she's separated from her body. I can't help but feel her tumbling shock. Alex's face flashes in my head. This time, I realize, I'm the perpetrator.

A shadow steps out from behind Hollie. It's Mom, a bag of pretzels nestled in the crook of her elbow, a vending machine snack I'm sure she bought to make me feel better. Now her face is rigid, her eyes pointed.

"Maxine," she says, "you apologize right now."

I blink, the world continuing to swirl.

"I—I'm sorry," I say. "I'm really sorry."

"It's okay," Hollie whispers, but she's backing out of the locker room.

Her footsteps hurry down the hall.

Mom careens toward me, her hands on her hips. "What has gotten into you?"

I stare down at my feet, but she tilts my chin upward, forcing me to look at her.

"In this family," she says, "we don't act like that."

"I'm sorry," I mumble.

Mom shakes her head. "I don't care if you've had a bad skate, Maxine." She pushes the pretzels into my hands. "It's no excuse to treat people unkindly."

She sighs. My body feels like it's shriveling into a prune. I wish I could disappear.

Icy Apologies

I toss and turn all night, and when at last I fall asleep, Kristi Yamaguchi emerges in my dreams. I'm sitting on a rubber floor, cross-legged, and she's on the ice, spinning toward me, a wide smile on her face. She's draped by a white background and nothing else: just her, the ice, and me. But when she gets closer, she frowns and shakes her head.

"I'm sorry," I say, staring down at my skates.

When I look up, she's gone.

It is just white, white, white. I reach out to touch the ice, but no matter how far I stretch my fingertips, I can't reach it. I am about to give up when a girl floats through the nothingness on a blue glass cloud, hovering above the ice, breaking the endless white. She's sitting cross-legged, too.

It's Hollie, I realize. Her cloud dips down to my feet.

"I'm sorry," I tell her, and I mean it this time.

Her eyes crinkle. "It's okay," she says.

But even my dream self knows it's not.

Beep! Beep! Beep!

My alarm cracks open my dream and I squint, adjusting to the light. It's seven in the morning. In just a few hours, I'll be back at the rink for my free skate. *It's a new day*, I tell myself. *Clean ice, clean start. You got this, Maxine.*

I can feel the bruise on my tailbone from yesterday's fall as I swing my legs off the bed. I wince as I press a hand to the tender spot. Maybe Mom can rub some Tiger Balm on it. Tiger Balm fixes everything. I curl my toes against the hardwood floor. In my bedroom mirror, I can still see smudges of makeup rimming my eyes from yesterday's disaster.

I wipe the back of my hand so vigorously against my skin that my cheekbone briefly swells red.

As I hustle downstairs, I smell crispy bacon and buttermilk pancakes on the griddle. There's a protein-packed smoothie already waiting for me on the counter. More fuel for regionals.

Mom is hunched over the newspaper, her elbows on the counter, reading glasses perched on the bridge of her nose. Dad stands over the stove in his pajamas. He tosses me a tentative smile. I know they had *quite* the chat last night. I could hear them whispering through the walls.

Dad dishes bacon and pancakes onto a plate, and slides it over to me. I take it, scooting onto a kitchen stool.

"Thanks," I say, and then, with Mom still staring at the newspaper and Dad's back to me, I gulp. Time to be a real *intermediate lady*, Maxine.

"I feel awful about yesterday."

I look down at my food. Mom's glasses peek out from behind the newspaper.

"I hope so," she says. "Although I don't think I'm the one you need to be telling that to."

I bite my lip. "I'll talk to Hollie at the rink today."

"Good." Mom folds the newspaper and tucks it under her arm. "I talked to her mom on the phone this morning."

I sit up. "What?"

Mom snatches a slice of bacon from the plate and takes a bite. "We've arranged a playdate for you two."

"A . . . *playdate?*"

I flash back to when I was six and used to sit in the living room with Victoria, dumping all my Barbies on the floor so that we could undress and redress them until we got bored. My chest hitches when I realize I haven't talked to her in weeks.

"A get-together. A hangout. Whatever."

Dad looks at me and shrugs. So this wasn't just a *chat*. Mom has built the ship and is clearly intent on sailing it to whichever sea she chooses. We are all getting on board.

"You girls barely know each other," she continues, "and I think it would do you some good to try."

I swallow a piece of pancake. "I'm not sure Hollie wants to hang out with me."

"She just moved here a couple of weeks ago. From what her mom says, she doesn't have any friends yet, Maxine."

Oh. I guess I didn't think about that. My shoulders droop.

"Okay."

Mom nods her head, like we've made a deal.

"Okay." She smiles, her hands on her hips. "Now finish your food. You've got a big day ahead of you."

Jennie

The junior girls are mesmerizing. The metal bleachers stick to the back of my legs as I lean forward, watching their every move. Mom drove me to the rink early so I could collect myself before the free skate. Sometimes it's calming to watch the older skaters finish up on the rink. The last handful of girls are warming up before their short program routines.

With powerful yet dainty legs, they speed around one another in circles before taking off into triple Lutzes and triple flips. As they fly, their dresses swing and spin in a dazzling pageant. None of the other intermediate girls are here yet, so it's just them and me.

Jennie Kim glides by with a smooth black bun and an emerald-green dress. Her blades click against the ice, her eyes so focused she's practically shooting laser beams. Kristi Yamaguchi may be my number one, but Jennie Kim is a very close second. She's from New York Skating Club in Manhattan, so I only see her at big competitions.

I follow her every move as she grabs her blade and lifts her right leg vertical to her left, almost parallel to her face. My eyes widen. She could be a trapeze artist.

When the junior girls are done warming up, I trail after them as they pile into the locker room. Even though it's the same room I saw yesterday, it's entirely transformed. Dresses swing from every hook, dozens and dozens, with complicated, delicate beading and deep mesh V-necks. Makeup is strewn across the benches, brushes rolling onto the floor. And to think, I thought *middle school* beauty routines were intense.

Jennie is huddled in the corner, a compact mirror inches from her face as she powders her cheeks. I touch my oily forehead. Should I be powdering, too?

That's when Jennie catches my eye, peeking out from behind the compact. I'm sure she's pinpointed my chipped nail polish and childish fuchsia fleece.

My cheeks burn. *Stupid Maxine, stupid Maxine, STUPID.* Thank God no one can see me blush through my tan skin. This is basically the only instance where I'm grateful to be Asian.

And then Jennie does something strange. Her hand beckons me over. I look around, but there's no one else behind me. Jennie Kim wants to talk to *me.* I swallow. My hands in my pockets, I walk slowly toward her. She's still holding the compact, powder brush perched between her fingertips.

"I'm so sorry," I begin babbling, "I'm an intermediate, not a junior, and I know I'm not supposed to be here yet, or at all right now, but I like to get to the ice early and—"

"Dude!" Jennie laughs. "It's fine."

Up close, she is even more perfect than she seems on the ice. Maybe the powder is really working wonders, but her skin is radiant. Her brown eye shadow fades right below her brow bone, her liquid eyeliner effortlessly flicked.

"Your makeup looks really good," I blurt.

Could. You. Be. More. Embarrassing?! The last of my dignity curdles in my toes. But Jennie just smiles. She lowers her compact.

"Thanks," she says, eyeballing the locker room clock. "Do you want me to do yours? I have some time."

"What?"

"Your makeup." Jennie grabs the giant makeup bag resting beside her and holds it up like she's lifting Simba from *The Lion King*. "If you want, I could do it for you."

I plop myself down on the bench before she can change her mind.

"Sure," I manage to squeak out.

"Cool."

Jennie waves a canister of foundation in my face.

"Liquid's the best kind," she instructs, "and Fenty has the most shades."

I always use Mom's foundation for competitions, but hers is an unsightly mixture of decades-old mustard yellow and muddy brown. I never put too much on. Otherwise it looks like I smeared my face with a dirty diaper wipe. Jennie's foundation, though, blends into my skin perfectly.

As if she can read my mind (I wouldn't be surprised, given all her other talents), Jennie says, "This is perfect since we have the same skin tone."

She pumps the foundation onto the back of her

hand and dabs it with a sponge before patting it on my face. My hands tingle. It feels like art class, except I'm the canvas. Then she pulls out another palette and swirls a big brush into bronzer.

"Suck in your cheeks like this," she says, her skin taut against her cheekbones.

I giggle. "Fish face."

"Yeah, exactly." She angles the brush and presses it into the crevices of my cheeks, drawing thin lines before blending with her brush.

"Where did you learn to do all this?" I marvel as she fills in my eyebrows with sticky black goop.

She shrugs, her shoulders shifting against her velvet sleeves. She flicks open the most dazzling eye shadow palette I've ever seen. It shimmers under the fluorescent lights.

"YouTube videos, mostly."

I perk up. "I watch beauty YouTubers, too!"

Jennie swirls a small brush into deep purple eye shadow. "Oh yeah? Which ones?"

I rattle a couple off the top of my head, but Jennie scrunches her nose as I ramble.

"Those ones are fine," she says, gently pressing my eyelids closed to sweep on the eye shadow, "but you should really watch the Asian makeup gurus."

I feel my goopy brows furrow as I sit in the dark.

"Don't do that," Jennie says, "you'll mess up your eye shadow."

"Sorry," I say.

"Yeah, Mascara_Mimi is my favorite. And then probably BubbleTeaAndBeauty."

I grin as Jennie slowly paints liquid eyeliner onto my lash line. It tickles. "Does BubbleTeaAndBeauty also do bubble tea tutorials?"

"No," she says with a chuckle, "but sometimes she reviews flavors."

"Jasmine is obviously the best."

Jennie coats mascara onto my eyelashes. "Are you crazy? Matcha all the way. You can open your eyes now."

The world becomes color again: Jennie's glowing

face smirking, a twinkle in her espresso irises. She flips open her compact and hands it to me.

"Ta-da," she says. "You look beautiful."

I stare at my reflection. I've never seen myself look like this before. Not that I look like a different person, but I just seem more luminous. My cheekbones are like silver knives, ready to slice the ice. My eyebrows are fierce and defined. But it's my eyes that make me gasp. Somehow, Jennie has brushed on the eye shadow at such an angle that it complements the paper-thin lines of my almond eyes. The eyeliner flicks upward with the natural corners of my skin. My eyes don't seem small anymore. Or wide, either. They just look . . . nice.

"Thank you," I breathe. "You're a wizard."

Jennie pats my head. "Watch those Asian makeup gurus," she says.

She grabs the compact from my fingers and gestures to the door. "All right, kiddo, I gotta go stretch."

I nod, and follow her out of the locker room. But

I'm still thinking about my eyes. My eyes, my eyes, the lids I hate so much, their shriveled curves, the ugly slits. Now they are almost pretty.

You look beautiful, Jennie said.

Maybe, I think. *Maybe more than almost.*

Ready or Not

"Eagle wings, all right, Maxine?" Judy whispers in my ear, her parka pressed against my shoulder as I stand at the rink's edge.

"Yep." I suck in the cold air. "I know."

The other intermediate girls turn in circles on the ice like ballerinas in a music box, twisting around one another during warm-up. As expected, Hollie is in blush pink for her Celine Dion free skate. Skating backward, she extends her right leg into a double Lutz, double loop. Perfection.

I roll my shoulders and stretch out my arms,

weaving in between the other skaters. Eagle wings, indeed.

The faster the girls around me move, the easier they blur, until only Hollie remains in focus, the gauzy skirt of her dress flapping against her thighs. Mom's comment this morning rattles around in my head: *I don't think I'm the one you need to be telling that to.* A mirage of Hollie's eyes prickled with tears skates across my vision—lips parted in shock, dream-Hollie floating toward me with hollow cheeks. I shake my head and focus on curving into a layback. If I bother her now, we could collide, and that would be *really* bad.

I skate until my legs are warm and tingly.

"Two minutes left," the loudspeaker booms.

Judy nods at me from across the rink.

I've had a good warm-up. Now I just have to repeat it when it really counts.

Judy paces at the boards, rubbing her hands

together. We both know how important this free skate is. She won't vocalize it because she doesn't want to stress me out. But I need an incredible score to jump to fourth place from seventh to qualify for sectionals. Otherwise, my season ends here.

We file off the ice one by one. The other girls stretch their legs over the boards and practice their landings on the mat until the announcer calls their names. But I trail after Hollie until we are just steps apart. Now's my chance. I reach out a hand and tap her gently on the shoulder.

"Hey," I say.

She turns, her green eyes blinking. "Hi," she says, and then, cocking her head at me: "Your makeup looks pretty."

I smile, remembering my reflection in Jennie's compact, the way the purple eye shadow gleamed.

"Thanks," I say. "Jennie did it."

Hollie's face lights up. "She's so cool."

"Yeah." I nod. "She is."

She glances down at her skates. I fiddle with my tights, flicking the fabric against my skin like a rubber band.

"So I just wanted to, uh, I just wanted to . . . to . . ."

Hollie steps backward, hugging her elbows.

"I—I—I'm really sorry. For yesterday." My words falter.

Hollie shifts her gaze from the floor to my face. "You already apologized. It's—"

I cut her off. "No, you never did anything to me and I was really—I wasn't—I was being mean. I'm sorry."

I keep snapping the fabric against my leg until it stings.

"You don't have to say it's okay," I quickly add.

A hint of a smirk emerges on Hollie's lips. She relaxes her shoulders.

"Okay," she says. "I mean, it's *not okay*." Hollie smiles.

I can't help but smile back.

"Good. I mean, great."

"Well, I guess we'll be seeing more of each other," she says as she smooths down the pleats in her dress, "now that our moms planned a *playdate* for us."

"Yeah," I say, "like we're four. Maybe we should play Barbies."

"On the playground."

"Better yet, in the sandbox."

"Supervised, *of course*."

"Oh, absolutely."

I smirk, and Hollie's eyes twinkle before we both burst into laughter. She holds her rib cage, clutching her dress's beaded bodice.

"Well," she says, "we should probably get back to it."

"Right," I say. "Good luck out there."

"You, too."

Hollie disappears into the locker room just as Judy runs out dangling an exercise band in one hand.

"Maxine," she says, "you ready?"

I push a loose strand of hair behind my ears and steady my feet in my skates.

"Yeah," I say, "I'm ready."

The Results Are In

The edge of the bench in the Kiss and Cry digs into the inside of my knees. My crystal-blue dress and gauzy tights are soaked with sweat. Judy hands me a towel to wipe off my forehead. Then she throws an arm around my shoulder, and I lean into her, rapidly swallowing the cold rink air.

"You did great, kid," she says, and I know she means it.

It's programs like these that I can hardly remember. The Gershwin piano keys flooded the rink and then it was just me and my skates. Every turn felt tight, every jump precise. But was it enough? I watch my rib cage expand and contract with the jewels stitched across my chest. In and out, in and out.

Right now, Katarina is in first and Fleur is in second. My base technical element score was higher than both of theirs—my jumps were more complicated and better executed. Katarina's artistry and choreography were killer, though, so she'll most likely receive a higher program component score than me.

There are only two skaters left, Hollie and Gwen, and if they skate clean, they'll probably win gold and silver. That means if I can just beat out Fleur, I'll be in fourth. I'll make sectionals.

I can't see Mom and Dad, but I know they are antsy in the bleachers, trying not to talk about every element in my free skate, but definitely giving in and talking about every element in my free skate.

That was a solid triple toe, right? I imagine them whispering.

Right, so positive grade of execution there.

Maybe we should replay it on your video camera just to make sure.

No, no, the judges have it handled.

But it'll only take ten seconds! We'll just check the triple toe, that's it.

Isn't that Fleur's mom over there? Go talk to her and distract yourself.

Don't change the subject.

Okay, fine, I'll check. Jeez.

Wait, *was* my triple toe fully rotated? No, I won't fall into this trap. I keep my eyes on the monitor. Shawn Mendes screams through the speakers. They always try to distract the crowd with punchy music while the judges compile the numbers. As much as I love his songs, his belting feels like earsplitting squeals now.

Is this how Karen Chen felt after her long program

at the 2018 US Championships? Her performance defined whether she or Ashley Wagner would make the Olympic team since Bradie Tennell and Mirai Nagasu were in first and second. I picture Karen in her all-black ensemble, defiant red lipstick, a giant burgundy flower pinned to her bun, as if to say: *I'm better. I'm stronger. I'll clinch this spot.* And she did.

I square my shoulders. *I'm better. I'm stronger. I'll clinch this spot.*

Numbers flash onto the monitor below my feet. A disembodied voice thunders over the PA.

"The scores, please, for Maxine Chen."

Judy squeezes my hand.

"For her performance, she has earned a score of 72.56 for a total score of 105.57. She is currently in second place."

My hands fly to my mouth and I fight the urge to jump to my feet. I can hear Mom shrieking with joy and sense Dad's fist flying into the air. Judy throws me into a giant embrace.

"You did it, girl. You're going to sectionals!"

I'm going to sectionals. I, Maxine Chen, am going to SECTIONALS. Tiny tears trickle down my cheeks. Sometimes, there are happy cries in the Kiss and Cry.

Cannon Fire

There should be a rule that after a big competition, I get the whole following week to lie on my bed, limbs outstretched like a starfish, and do absolutely nothing. Mom, unfortunately, does not agree with me. On Monday morning, she makes me do my usual twenty crunches and then pushes my very sore legs out the door and down the hill to school. Now I'm sitting in the library yawning every three minutes while blinking at a computer screen. At least I got to sleep in. Judy said I deserved a three-day break from morning practice. This is the first morning in months that I've woken up on a weekday with the sun streaming through my window.

Mr. Warren is rattling off a series of best research practices, but his voice crackles against my ears like radio static. I look at my fingertips. I can still feel the touch of the cool pewter of the fourth-place medal, now proudly hanging on a hook in our living room next to a Polaroid Dad snapped from my free skate.

Hollie won gold, like I knew she would. She really did skate beautifully. I still stand by the fact that Celine Dion is cheesy, though.

Crack! I am jolted out of my daydreams by what sounds like someone taking a fist to their keyboard. I turn, the ice and Celine Dion melting before my eyes. Instead, I find Alex pounding on his keyboard—a library performance for the boys laughing beside him.

I glare as he smashes the keys, a heavy-bellied snort escaping from his lips. Today, his spiky hair situation is at an all-time high. Literally. I am convinced that there's a porcupine growing on his head.

I wish I could tell him how stupid he looks, how infantile, but my body still feels small and empty around him. Instinctively, I want to curl into a corner.

"Alex Macreesy," Mr. Warren's voice thunders, jumping by six decibels, "have you ever heard of the phrase, 'You break it, you buy it'?"

Alex glances up at Mr. Warren's puffed-out chest. "Huh?"

"You break it, you buy it," Mr. Warren repeats, stepping forward. "If you break that keyboard, I will personally send your parents the bill. Understood?"

Alex's cheeks turn the color of ripe strawberries. He slumps down in his seat, his porcupine head drooping. I didn't even know Alex had the capacity to feel embarrassed. The realization almost makes me feel powerful, strong. Laughter builds, bubbling up to my nose. I can't help it. I let out a snicker.

Alex's eyes whiz toward mine, sharp and ugly.

His face is still blotchy, but his fists ball up like he's waiting to punch me in the gut. Okay, I totally take back that snicker now.

Mr. Warren turns around to help Elisa. Alex's friends squirm in their seats, pretending to be thoroughly engrossed in their research. I try to focus on my computer screen.

Paragraphs on paragraphs about Mary Ludwig Hays loom before me. I yawn. Why is she important again?

I scroll through a couple of articles, too lazy to move my hand from the mouse and read anything. Then I stop. In one illustration, there's a battle scene showing a woman with curly brown hair stuffed under a cap, soot covering her cheeks, shoving a cannonball or something into the mouth of a cannon. Soldiers have fallen on the scorched grass beneath her feet. In another, she's shown jamming some kind of pole down the barrel. Whatever it is, she definitely knows what she's doing with it. The caption below the painting says: *A depiction of Mary Ludwig Hays at the Battle of Monmouth.*

I keep reading. *At the Battle of Monmouth in June 1778, Mary Ludwig Hays helped the soldiers by offering them water and supplies. The weather was extremely hot. Mary's husband and fellow soldier, William Hays, collapsed during the battle. As he was carried off the field, Mary quickly took his place at the cannon and continued to "swab and load" using her husband's ramrod. During the battle, a British cannonball came right at her and tore off part of her skirt. She is believed to have responded, "Well, that could have been worse," and carried on fighting.*

There are more images of Mary with a giant wheeled cannon, fiercely concentrating as the other men around her battle on, an American flag billowing in the background. After the war, George Washington apparently honored Mary by officially making her a noncommissioned officer. From then on, she went by her nickname, "Sergeant Molly," and was called that for the rest of her life.

I stare at the computer, eyes fastened to Mary's

torn skirt and clenched fists, her determination as she defied expectations and fought the British. I know *exactly* what scene I'm writing for the skit. Maybe Dad can build me one of those cool cannon-blaster things. I cock my head at the giant wheels that probably would be as tall as I am. Well, I don't know how we're going to make *those*. But details, details.

"Psst, Maxine."

Mitchell Hawkins smiles at me from behind his mass of red hair. I glance at him, and then at the other two boys also looking at me, their necks craned my way. In the middle sits Alex. He's grinning at his computer screen, which is tilted my way. And then looking straight at me, he presses his index finger on the keyboard button to scroll down to a message that fills his screen in huge bold font.

MAXINE
IS A
NERDY
CHINK!

Mitchell and Alex and the other boys start cracking up, covering their mouths with their hands to stifle their laughter. I wish I could be somewhere else. Anywhere else.

Mr. Warren senses the commotion from across the room and stands up. Alex whips around in his seat, quickly deleting all the evidence. It's as if his words never existed, even though I can't stop seeing them.

Keep it together, Maxine, I try to tell myself, but the words *nerdy chink* ring in my ears until I'm nauseous.

Alex and his friends are still laughing as they zip up their backpacks.

The bell rings.

I am not a nerd, I think, *I am not a nerd, but I am a chink. I am a chink. I am—*

I clench my eyes shut and think hard about Jennie, cooler and smarter than everyone in this stupid room. I focus on her perfect smoky eye shadow, chin held high, Asian and proud. I try to imagine myself that way, like I felt that moment wearing purple eye shadow, staring into her compact mirror. But I can't find that Maxine. She's not here right now.

I open my eyes. Purple eye shadow can make my eyes pop, but it doesn't change who I am. Not to Alex, at least.

And maybe not even to me.

Pretending

"There's my sectionals lady!"

Mom swings open the car door, cupping my flushed cheeks in her hands. I tumble inside. After school, I walked to the rink and did Lutz after Lutz until I couldn't anymore. Thankfully, Judy was busy helping Sam with his sit spins and Fleur was moping about her fifth-place finish, so no one bothered me today. In the silence, I flung my body into the air until Alex and the computer screen and the flashing words disintegrated beneath the ice.

But now, looking out at the shadow of mountains curved beneath the skyline, the whole day floods my mind once more. I avoid Mom's abundant cheer as I buckle my seat belt. The car ride home takes only a few minutes, so at least I won't have to endure her giddiness for too long. Mom turns on the stereo. Sappy string music blasts from the speakers and Teresa Teng's tinny voice fills the car. She's singing something in Mandarin I can't understand.

"Can you turn that down?" I grumble.

Mom raises an eyebrow.

"Sure," she says, adjusting the dial, and then: "What's with the mood? Was everyone at school happy for you?"

Ha. Like I told anyone at school about regionals.

"Yeah, Mom, they were."

"Victoria must be so proud of you."

When Victoria's not clinging to Alex, she's flocked by theater kids anxiously discussing this year's musical. This morning, I could hear her shriek from twenty feet away when she looked at the cast list and realized she got the role of Nancy in *Oliver!* Little does she know that I peeked at the list, too, just to see if she nabbed the part. Not that I'm going to congratulate her or anything. She doesn't even acknowledge me in the cafeteria anymore.

"Uh-huh."

"Do you have a lot of homework to catch up on? Is that it? You know Dad and I can help you."

"No, I'm all set."

"And practice? It went well?"

I look out the window. "It was fine."

Mom sighs, weary eyes on the road as she turns onto our street. Teresa's voice, now quiet, runs up the octave.

"Okay," Mom finally says.

I know there is so much she wants to say. There is so much I want to say. But if I tell her anything, she'll call the principal or the superintendent or— knowing her—ring up the PTA and give all the parents a lecture, and then I'll be the laughing-stock of Mirror Lake Middle School. *Maxine called her mommy because she couldn't deal with a little teasing.* I can just hear their cackles now. I can just see

Victoria and Alex, arms linked as they skip down the hallway, shaking their heads at stupid, nerdy Maxine. The *chink*.

As we turn into our driveway, Mom studies my face.

"You're sure you're okay?" She taps my chin and smiles.

I force myself to smile back.

"Yeah," I tell her, "don't worry."

A Little TLC

On Friday after school, Hollie shows up on my doorstep wearing pajama pants covered in little orange pumpkins and a *Skater Girl* sweatshirt. Her wavy hair is piled on top of her head in a messy bun. She points to her bottoms.

"'Cause of Halloween on Sunday. Get it?"

I swing open the front door a little wider to reveal my own skeleton sweatpants and black cat slippers. We both smile.

It's kind of insane that my former archnemesis is legitimately standing in my foyer right now, looking around at photos of my family, snapshots of seven-year-old me in flouncy costumes and too much lipstick, proudly showing off my medals. Most of them are silver or bronze. I bet all the ones in Hollie's house are *gold*.

I take a deep breath. Mom gave me a whole lecture this morning about collaboration, not competition, and keeping rivalry strictly on the ice. Then she went into some whole long story about this girl she used to hate who was her opponent in badminton and how they grew up and became friends and went to each other's weddings, blah, blah, blah. Sometimes, I think Mom tries to wear me out just by talking a lot.

Anyway, I figure that Nathan Chen and Yuzuru Hanyu are always pitted against each other in competition, and they're both nice to each other. Or at least, they compliment each other during press conferences. So maybe I can do this, too.

Hollie follows me into the kitchen. My eyes immediately jump to the little Buddha nestled in the corner by the jar of chopsticks, and the scroll on the wall Dad inherited from Grandpa that says a bunch of Chinese proverbs I don't understand. When Victoria came over last year, she told me that my house smelled weird. What if Hollie goes back to the rink and tells Fleur and Sam and everyone else that my house is a total freak show? I swallow a lump in my throat and remember to breathe. To calm myself down, I play Would You Rather in my head:

Would you rather Hollie or Victoria be here?

Hollie or *Alex*?

I think about his stupid porcupine head.

Hollie. Definitely Hollie.

If Hollie thinks anything about my house, she doesn't show it. Instead, she gravitates toward the brownie mix Mom left on the counter for us, cradling the box like a newborn baby.

"Chocolate fudge brownies are my favorite," she says. She's practically jumping up and down. It's like she's never seen brownie mix before.

"Cool," I say, "let's make 'em."

While the oven preheats, I grease a baking pan, and Hollie dumps the mix into a bowl and adds oil and water. As she stirs, I squeeze in the little packet of fudge. I have no idea what to say to Hollie, who keeps sniffling and quietly humming to herself. The silence is earsplitting. I can literally hear Mom flipping magazine pages in the living room.

I scoop an egg out of the carton, trying not to break it. Hollie concentrates intensely on our concoction, her mouth moving quietly. Notes escape from her lips.

I freeze, about to crack the egg against the rim of the bowl.

"Are you singing . . . 'No Diggity'?"

Hollie's head shoots up, her face bright pink.

"Uh," she says, "no?"

I shake my head at her. "Yes, you are!"

"Okay, I know it's weird," she blurts, "but I just really like the old stuff. Like Destiny's Child, and the Spice Girls, and Usher, and all of that because I went into a Beyoncé black hole one time and just became really invested."

She smooshes her hands against her cheeks and stares at me with worried eyes.

"Don't laugh at me." Then her expression changes. "Wait, how do *you* know that song?"

A smirk tugs at the corners of my lips. "Ummmmm, I also love nineties music."

"You do?"

My singing voice sounds like a cat wailing, but I manage to croak out the first few lines of TLC's "No Scrubs."

Hollie smiles so wide I think I can see every single one of her braces. She shimmies as I sing, bopping her shoulders up and down and twisting her arms like spaghetti. I let out a snort.

"You're kind of weird," I say between hiccups

of laughter. I crack the egg open and add it to the mix.

Hollie sticks out her tongue at me, turning back to the bowl and the batter.

"So are you."

A Light Bulb Goes Off

One kitchen karaoke session of all the Spice Girls' greatest hits later, we bring our baked treat upstairs and sprawl out on my bedroom floor. Hollie stretches her pumpkin pajama legs and hops to her feet, checking out my spinner and weights and every poster covering my walls. She points to Nathan Chen on the ceiling.

"I like this one the best."

I nod, cross-legged on my paisley rug. I mean, who *wouldn't* want the first and last thing they see every day to be the ever-perfect Nathan Chen with his easy smile and dozens of medals?

Hollie sighs. "His hair is so floppy," she says.

"Agreed."

She moves to my desk, eyeing the algebra home-work scattered across its surface, the Quiz Bowl participation ribbons haphazardly pushpinned to the bulletin board. Her shoulders sag.

"I wish I were in school," she says, like she's wish-ing for a trip to Disney World or Hawaii instead of a visit to hell on earth.

I sit forward, wiping brownie crumbs onto my leggings.

"You don't go to *school*?"

Suddenly, this majestic life billows before me, one without stupid boys and friends that are no longer your friends and lockers and homework you can't finish because you don't have enough time. No wonder Hollie is nailing her triple-double com-binations. I would, too, if I didn't have to see Alex Mac-greasy-face every day.

Hollie shakes her head. "Well, sort of. I'm home-schooled."

"Oh," I say.

No wonder she doesn't have any friends.

Hollie plops back onto the floor, tucking her ankles under her thighs. She looks almost . . . sad.

"Have you always been homeschooled?" My voice comes out in a whisper.

"No," she says, "not until skating became really intense. Then Mom pulled me out to focus on competing." She traces a flower on my rug. "It's been almost four years since I've been in real school."

"Wow."

Hollie shrugs. "It's okay. I mostly just do work-books and they're pretty easy." She pauses. "It's just a little lonely, you know? My younger brother is two years old, so there's not really anyone for me to talk to."

"Well, aren't your parents around?"

"Only my mom," Hollie says, "and she can be . . . a lot." Hollie turns her face toward the window. "She really wants me to focus. To work hard and get to nationals. And when I'm old enough, the international circuit. And then one day . . . well . . ."

Hollie holds out her arms like she's trying to contain the entire world.

"The Olympics," I finish.

"Yeah. The Olympics. I guess it's just a lot of pressure."

She glances back at me, her eyes scanning my face, searching for understanding.

"I get it," I say, but I don't, really.

I *do* want to go to the Olympics, but it's a want, not a need. For Hollie, it seems different. I think about Mom and Dad, always worried that there's too much on my plate, assuring me that I can quit when I want to, insisting that I work hard but also make time for fun. And brownies. I sink my teeth into chocolaty fudge.

Hollie starts telling me about her days—stretches of alone time on the ice, just her and the music, her skates slicing this way and that across the frozen surface. She says that she tries to sneak in reading between sessions. Her eyes light up when she talks about fantasy novels filled with long-lost queens: girls who travel through imaginary worlds and giant monsters with scales and long, bloody fangs. In Virginia, she used to climb up and hide in the oak tree in her backyard and read until her mom found her. Now she huddles in a window seat flanked by bay windows, looking out onto Mirror Lake.

"That sounds really nice," I tell her, and I mean it. Stealing time to do anything extra like read or paint is rare. When I'm not skating, I'm at school, or crouched in the corner of Bob's Skate Shop, rushing to finish problem sets before practice begins.

"Yeah," she says, "sometimes it is. But what about you? What's school like?" She leans forward, like I'm going to tell her about another magical world from one of her books.

My mind immediately swirls with memories of Alex's sneer, his neck craned toward me in the library, bold black letters on white, white, white:

chink. His laughter. I try to fight the tears pricking my eyes, but they dot my lashes anyway. Great. Now I'm officially a wuss in front of my former-archnemesis-maybe-friend who barely knows me, much less wants to see me cry about a dumb boy.

Hollie's shoulders straighten. "Are you okay?"

"Oh," I say, my voice tight and squeaky, "yeah."

Geez. Good thing I'm a skater, not an actor. I'd be a total failure.

Hollie's hair whips across her face as she shakes her head.

"I'm not buying it."

She stares at me, green eyes so wide I worry they'll explode if I don't say something. So I tell her.

"It's just this boy at school," I say. My eyes drift to the floor, fingers now mimicking Hollie's as I trace the rug's flowers, back and forth, back and forth.

"Ooh, like a crush?"

"No. NO." I pause, inhaling sharply. "His name is Alex. And he's kind of a jerk. A *big* jerk. Well, it's stupid that I even care, but he . . . he always makes fun of me and, like, well, he says things about me being Asian, or *Chinese* to be exact, I guess, and it makes me . . . it makes me feel really awful."

Hollie is still looking at me, but she's quiet.

I close my eyes. I've made a terrible mistake.

I can already hear her glossed lips whispering through the rink's walls: *Not only did Maxine barely make sectionals, but she's also a total loser at school. What a joke.*

I wish I could leave, but this is my own freaking room. I look up at the ceiling. Nathan stares back at me, utterly useless. I guess floppy hair can't help me now.

Hollie pulls her feet from underneath her thighs and sits cross-legged, mirroring me.

"I'm really sorry, Maxine," she says. "He sounds terrible."

I glance up at her still-wide eyes. I think she *genuinely* feels sorry for me.

"Could you say something to him? To make him shut up?"

I shake my head. "I try, but I freeze every time."

"But you're so confident," Hollie says, her arms now flailing in my face, "like when I see you on the rink or at ballet or whatever, you look so powerful and awesome—and cool." Patches of pink crawl up her cheeks. "I really admire that about you."

"You do?"

"Yeah!" Hollie grins.

Huh. I never really thought about the way I appear to everyone else at the rink. But Hollie's right—I am confident on the ice, much more than at school. After all, I practice so much that skating becomes second nature to me.

A megawatt lightbulb flashes in my brain and I jump to my feet. Hollie's eyes trail upward, concerned.

"Wait, maybe I can *practice* saying things back to Alex, and that way the next time he's being terrible, I'll be prepared."

Hollie holds her chin in her hands, like she's really considering my idea.

"That makes sense," she finally answers, "like you could write up some comebacks."

I smile, for real this time. "Exactly."

I find an old history work sheet on my desk and flip it over, pen poised.

"Okay," I say, "we need to come up with insults."

"Maybe first you should write down what he's said to you"—Hollie crosses her arms over her chest, cradling her elbows—"so you know exactly what to say back."

"Right." I touch my pen to paper. My hand shakes when I write out the words *NERDY CHINK* slowly, and in big letters at the top of the page. I hate that I remember every insult, every sneer. They flow out of me like water and I write them all down: *Your eyes are too big in your painting. But you people are good at math. Can't you just be useful?* I add a couple more Alex would probably say. Hollie peers over my shoulder as I scribble furiously.

"Man," she says, "this dude is a total blockhead."

I laugh. "Yeah, he is."

Hollie points at the math insult. "You could say something like: I'll make myself useful when you add up to something more than useless."

"Okay," I say, "that was pretty good."

"If he says your eyes are too small, you should say: Well, they're big enough to see that you're an idiot!" She giggles.

I snicker and write it down. But as I stare at the page, the word *CHINK* glares at me, unwilling to disappear.

"What about this?" I say, pointing to the word I dare not repeat: "It rhymes with *THINK*, which is more than a loser like you can do."

Hollie excitedly clasps her hands together. "Your jokes are so dumb because your IQ is so low."

"Nice! Maybe: Where am I *really* from? Well, where are *you* from? The corner of Ugly Street and Racist Alley?"

Now we're whipping up a sweet batch of

comebacks, faster than I can write them down. Our back and forth gets louder and sillier and sillier, until we are doubled over, laughing so hard that our ribs hurt. Hollie is pretty much rolling around on my rug.

There's a knock at the door. Mom peers inside, holding a steaming plate of dòu shā bāo—pillowy-soft red bean buns. She looks shocked.

"You girls good in here?"

I nod, happily snatching the buns from her hands.

"Couldn't be better."

Dance It Out

Is it just me, or is the ice gleaming? The Zamboni guy must have done an excellent job today because I swear I can see glitter beneath my feet. As I zoom down the ice, I imagine my skates leaving behind a trail of sparks. I can't wait to use our new strategy for fighting back against Porcupine Head. The comebacks from yesterday wrap around me like armor. With the sweeping of my blades across the ice, I imagine swinging chain mail gauntlets at Alex, each counter more biting than the last. The next time he sneers, I'll be ready.

"Lookin' good, Max." Fleur sidles up to me, blowing loose strands of hair from her face.

I T-stop as she leans her arm against my shoulder. "Thanks, girl." I grin, glad she's no longer moping. When Fleur's upset, the rink becomes a scary episode of *Don't Talk to Fleur, She'll Murder You: The Reality Show*. But with regionals in the past, she's back to her chipper, gossipy self.

"Maxine!" Judy waves to me from the boards.

I squint. There's someone standing next to her. I say good-bye to Fleur and skate closer, making out the stranger's thick black hair. A woman in a painted-gold scarf offers me a closemouthed smile.

"Maxine, this is Meghana," Judy says, "your new ice dance coach."

"New coach?" I squeak.

Judy laughs. "Don't worry, I'm not going anywhere." She fishes around in her pockets, emerging with a crumpled score chart that she promptly waves in my face. "Your program components were not exactly where we wanted them, so your parents and I decided you could use a couple of ice dance sessions."

I gulp. Are my edges really that bad that I need an ice dance coach? How much did Mom and Dad shell out for this? As if Judy can read my mind, she whispers in my ear: "You're in the big leagues now, Maxine. Time to step up your game."

My head bobs up and down, my mind running with mirages of Karen Chen and Jennie Kim with a cat eye so sharp it could slice the ice. Each girl on the brink of success, ready to flap their own eagle wings. I think of Alex and his pink mouth wide with laughter. Hollie and I had scrawled "Master Chen" on our comeback list. I inhale. Time to prove it.

"Okay," I say, my eyes moving from Judy to Meghana, "let's do this."

Meghana takes off her skate guards and follows me out to the center of the rink, Judy in her shadow. She cues up some peppy jazz on her phone and places it in her pocket so we have some music to work with.

Ice dance is more than just footwork and flowy movements; it's tight turns and twisting your body to the beats of the music. Meghana pushes her hair behind her ears and holds my arms out.

"Let's start with a basic chassé," she instructs.

She pulls my body left and right, mimicking my strokes as we dance across the ice. With her face inches away, I study her dark skin and deep brown eyes. I've never seen an Indian figure skater before, much less a coach. In fact, I could probably count on one hand the number of South Asians living in Lake Placid right now. Our little country town of shopkeepers is as white as the stars on the American flag. I hate that it makes people like Meghana and me feel like outsiders. But Meghana's focused on other things. She shakes her head at me.

"Point your foot," she says.

Ugh. She sounds just like Winona without the tiny claps and oozing pep.

"Good, now let's do it with your program music."

The song warbles from her phone as I swing my leg in circles, my hands flitting out by my sides.

We work on Choctaw turns next, followed by twizzles. I keep tilting and losing my balance, my foot twisting as I catch my fall and create little skid marks, piled with snow.

Judy sighs. Snow is a bad sign, I know. Meghana pushes on my skate, reminding me to put pressure on the center and heels of my feet, rather than the balls.

"Stay centered," she says.

Stay centered, I repeat to myself, running through comebacks until they spin upward, poised in my voice box, just waiting to escape. *Turn, turn, bunny hop, twizzle, tell Alex off.* My shoulders straighten with determination.

"Much better!" Meghana says.

We practice until the giant stadium seats are empty and darkness folds through the narrow line of windows tipping down from the ceiling. When we finally finish, my limbs feel like wooden puppet legs. I can't wait to crawl into bed.

That's when I see Hollie, just getting on the ice. I pull my phone out of my parka. It's almost nine p.m.

"Hey!" I call to her.

Hollie enthusiastically waves back. "Hi!"

She's strapped to a harness that's attached to a long pole, clutched by Viktor. He pushes her onto the ice. Harnesses are training tools that help skaters learn jumps beyond their skill level. I bite my lip. Hollie already has a triple Salchow and a triple toe under her belt. What is she doing next? Triple loops? Triple Lutzes? In *combination*? That would be wild. I inhale slowly. *Stay centered.*

Lo and behold, Viktor is yelling as Hollie skates on a back outside edge into a lopsided triple Lutz, followed by a messy double toe. Out of the corner of my eye, I can see her mom pacing along the rink's edge, lips pursed, trained on Hollie's every move. I think about what Hollie said about pressure. My heart sinks.

Outside, my mom is waiting in the car, headlights

flashing in the darkness. I buckle my seat belt and turn to her. She tucks a finger under my chin.

"So Meghana, huh? Was she helpful?"

I don't say anything, instead wrapping my arms around her waist in a tight hug. Mom's mouth parts into a tiny O.

"I'm going to take that as a yes."

I smile as the night sky blankets our windows. We drive forward.

America, America

MARY LUDWIG HAYS: Here's a jug of water to clean your rifles.

SOLDIER: Thanks, Mary!

[The battle is beginning. The British are shooting!]

MARY: Oh dear!

[She rushes to the sidelines.]

WILLIAM HAYS: Mary, stay out of the way!

[He is hit by a bullet and tumbles backward.]

MARY: William!

[She rushes to his side and wraps his wound tightly in gauze. His cannon is left unattended.]

[Mary makes a snap decision: She begins to
swab and load William's cannon.]

SOLDIER: Mary, what are you doing?

ANOTHER SOLDIER: You can't be doing that! It
is not a woman's job!

[Mary ignores them. A cannonball flies
between her legs, ripping part of her skirt.]

SOLDIER: Mary!

MARY: [Grins, dusting her hands off.] Well, that
could have been worse.

In the dim light of my bedroom, I put my pencil down with a groan. It's Halloween. I should be prancing around the neighborhood in a witch's costume, collecting cauldrons of candy. Instead, I'm here writing this terrible skit. I had practice all day today, so this is the only time I can work on it.

The doorbell rings.

"I'll get it!" Dad shouts.

I hear muffled voices floating up to my bedroom. Very high-pitched, giggly voices. Slowly, I tiptoe across the carpet and gently crack open the door. Over the banister, I see Victoria and three others in the doorway, illuminated in the porch light. Victoria's dressed as Dorothy from *The Wizard of Oz*, her long hair in ribboned pigtails, a plaid, puffy dress swinging against her knees. Her theater friends are the Scarecrow, Tin Man, and Lion. They hold out pillowcases and shiver in the cold.

"Victoria," Dad says, plopping Kit Kats into their bags, "so nice to see you."

"You, too, Mr. Chen," she replies, ever so polite. "Happy Halloween." No one would ever know that we aren't really friends anymore—except for the fact that I'm not out there with her, dressed as Toto or something. Guess she really *is* a good actress.

My fingers tighten around the doorknob.

"Maxine is upstairs," I hear Dad continue. "Do you want to say hi?"

"Oh, that's okay," Victoria is quick to respond. "I have to get home, and I don't want to bother her."

My stomach clenches tighter and tighter as she and her friends clamber down the steps.

"Have a good night, Mr. Chen!"

Dad closes the door. His head shifts toward my room, so I race back to my desk. Holding my breath, I listen as his footsteps get closer. A few seconds later, there's a knock on my door.

"Come in!"

"Hey," Dad says, a handful of Kit Kats in his palm. "I brought you something."

I can see how hard he's trying not to ask questions, how guilty he feels that I'm doing homework instead of trick-or-treating. It's not his fault. There's so much I want to tell him about Victoria and Alex, and how tired I am, but I don't know where to start. Instead, I push back my chair and let the Kit Kats fall into my hands.

"Thanks, Dad."

He ruffles my hair. "Good luck, kid."

When he leaves, I put my script to the side and

try to write Mary Ludwig Hays's biography, but I can't focus. Victoria and her ribboned pigtails crowd my brain. I curl my knees to my chest and press on the patches of Band-Aids covering my ankles. Lately, I've been getting blisters all the time. It probably means my skates are too small, but I can't risk buying new ones right now. It would take too long to break them in. Rolling my head backward, I pull out my phone. Since I'm clearly not getting any work done, I might as well look up cool 1700s hairstyles for tomorrow.

Uh, the girl's hair in one video is like the mane of a horse. It's so long you could make two wigs out of it. I pull at my own shoulder-length hair. Yeah, not going to happen. The best I *think* I can do is braid it and then maybe bobby-pin the tails to my head in a fake bun. I twist my hair into tight French braids. Ever since I started competing, Mom and I have had to do some sort of elaborate updo for my programs, pulling my hair this way and that to create tidy chignons that dare not move when I'm propelling my body two feet into the air. As a result, I've become a bit of a hair expert. Plus, I like braiding. It's relaxing—and an excellent form of procrastination.

I blink at my reflection in the mirror above my desk. At least I get to play a girl in my skit. Most of the "unsung heroes" are dudes. I decide to look up all the people Mr. Warren wrote on the board.

Henry Knox: Some white guy with an unfortunate shirt collar covering his neck.

Moses Brown: Some other white guy with a permanent frown etched onto his face.

Roger Sherman: Yet another white guy.

John Paul Jones: Are all the Revolutionary War heroes white guys?

At the end of my search, I have over a dozen tabs open to old portraits I've found—layer upon layer of grim men staring sternly into nothingness. My bleary eyes wash over their sallow skin. If you took snapshots of everyone who lived in Lake Placid—of Victoria and her pigtails, of her theater friends, of Alex and his spiky over-gelled hair, and then pressed their images over these paintings, they would all look the same—just like the founding fathers wanted.

I look back at my own skin, tawny and bronzed from the sun. I pull on the hollows of my cheeks, thinking about Jennie and Meghana—rubies in a sea of diamonds. Where do we fit in?

Putting on a Show

To think, last night I was carelessly braiding my hair like a colonist's and Googling old white dudes. Now, with my hair pinned, I can feel every bead of sweat trickling down my neck, my script shaking in my hands. Twenty-three bored faces turn toward me. This is *way* worse than a skating competition. Mr. Warren tugs on the ends of his mustache and nods at me encouragingly.

I hand him a copy of the script. "I'm going to need you to read the boy parts."

Someone sighs loudly, but I try to pretend it's

only Judy cheering me on as I complete a flawless triple toe.

"Of course, Maxine." His voice is gentle and soothing, like Dad's when he's persuading me to try ginger-soy fish or shrimp with the eyeballs still attached.

I chant Mom's saying in my head: *Shuǐ dī shí chuān.* "If you're persistent, you can overcome anything." And right now, I really need to overcome my stage fright or else I'll fail history and have to drop out of school or something. And I can't do *that* because I'm twelve. *You got this, Maxine.*

I run through my skit, enunciating every word like Mom and I practiced.

Mr. Warren proves himself a great soldier, indignantly bellowing that a *woman* such as myself can't possibly load a cannon. I pick up the ramrod that Dad and I put together last weekend, and pretend to defiantly swab and load an imaginary cannon until the British army falls to the ground. I then read through the rest of Mary's biography, talking about her legacy and bravery, and making sure to include dates and some details on what a ramrod is for and how you load a cannon so I can get extra points. When I'm finished, I let out a big lungful of air.

"Brava, brava!" Mr. Warren shouts, his mustache curved at the corners of his lips like a second smile.

The class offers loud applause. Elisa claps lightly, her red ponytail swinging as her hands come together. She's wearing fake pearls and a weird doily over her shirt as Abigail Adams.

"Thanks," I reply, wiping my forehead as I hurry back to my seat.

"Now, who's next?" Mr. Warren saunters around the "stage," a taped section of tile in front of the whiteboard.

"How about you, Mr. Macreesy? I believe the class has a lot to learn about"—he looks down at his paper—"John Laurens?"

The class turns to Alex. He sinks down in his

seat, so focused on digging his pencil into his desk that you'd think it was a school assignment.

"Alex?"

Mr. Warren walks down the rows slowly before he reaches Alex's slumped form. He taps the top of Alex's chair.

"Anyone in there?"

Porcupine Head jerks upward, his shoes squeaking against the floor. Elisa rolls her eyes, adjusting her doily collar.

"I don't have it," he mumbles into his sweatshirt.

"What was that?"

"I didn't write the stupid skit, okay?" Alex's voice cracks, echoing off the walls. Whispers and giggles snake through the aisles.

"What a doofus," someone says.

Elisa rubs her temples like she has a massive headache.

"All right, settle down," Mr. Warren says. He frowns at the class. Alex is seemingly immersed in the lettering on his blueberry sweatshirt.

"Tomorrow, Mr. Macreesy"—Mr. Warren's voice is stern—"I expect a full skit about John Laurens. Understood?"

"Yes," Alex mutters.

"Good."

When the bell finally rings, Alex springs to his feet, dumping all his books into his backpack faster than you can say *Revolutionary War*.

I hurtle toward the door, crammed behind throngs of classmates still snickering and gossiping.

Someone crashes into my back, jolting me forward. My skit, still crumpled in my hands, flutters to the ground. A shoe pushes off the page, a dirt-encrusted sneaker mark now caked onto my script. I spin around.

"Hey!"

Alex is standing behind me, beady eyes pointed right at mine as if he were a hawk ready to swoop in and snatch his prey.

He pokes my arm. "Mary's skin was white, not yellow," he whispers.

I flinch. The papers are still scattered on the floor, and I can feel myself sweating. But then I remember Hollie's face, aglow with fiery determination, with the belief that I am somehow wittier and smarter than the boy standing before me. *Practice makes perfect*, I tell myself. The cannon inside me prepares to fire. My voice says:

"Well, John Laurens was a soldier, not a swine. Oh, that's right, you wouldn't know since you're too stupid to even do the assignment."

The words fly from my mouth and explode into the air. Alex's eyes widen, and then—as the insult settles in—narrow once more. They begin to darken.

But he says nothing. Or rather, at last, he has nothing to say. Instead he pushes past me, knocking my shoulder so that I stumble.

This time, though, I catch my fall.

Victory

After school, I sprint across the front lawn and burst into the rink, searching the long maze of hallways with half-crazed eyes.

I run right into Fleur's mom, whose granola bar almost spills onto the floor.

"Maxine!" she shouts.

"Oops, sorry." I cringe, backing away slowly.

She's got on overalls and giant yellow earmuffs that make her look like a grown-up-size Minion. I stifle a giggle. She puts her hands on her hips.

"If you keep jumping around like that, you're going to hurt yourself. Then who will compete at sectionals?"

I bite my bottom lip. "Fleur?"

June's face widens in surprise before she smiles just a tiny bit.

"Does your mother know you're such a trouble-maker?"

I grin. "Yep."

She shakes her head before sauntering back down the hallway.

I jog past the synchro girls and the hockey players and the little kids at Learn to Skate classes before I dash up a stairway and keel over. Man, just because I skate does *not* mean I can run. I stop at the snack stand perched on the rink's balcony. Flopping my arms over the counter, I breathe in whiffs of hot grease and sugar. *Mmmm.* I can almost taste the crunchy sweetness. Mom and Dad rarely let me get snack stand food because it's "processed" and "bad for my health." I'm pretty much stuck on a diet of meat, healthy carbs, fruit, and vegetables. Mom always lectures that chips will make me sleepy on the ice and destroy my insides or something. But today, I dig around in my backpack for change and manage to find nine quarters total: just enough for my favorite guilty pleasure. If I can scarf them down in seven and a half minutes, I'll have plenty of time to warm up.

Cressie raises an eyebrow when she sees me.

"Miss Maxine, to what do we owe the pleasure of your stomping feet?"

I look up sheepishly. "Have you seen Hollie anywhere? I have very important news to tell her."

"Very important, huh? Well, you can tell an old lady, too. There's not much good gossip around here." She laughs, like she's the audience for her own joke.

I shake my head, my braids bopping against my neck. "Just school stuff," I say.

As if I would tell Cressie Oliver *anything*. Two weeks ago, she offhandedly told everyone that Jimmy (one of the junior boys) had a secret girlfriend, and then last week, we all found out that it was Donna, Adam's ice dance partner. Now they can't go anywhere without someone at the rink shouting, "Donna and Jimmy sitting in a tree!" Apparently, some things don't change no matter how old you are.

Cressie winks at me. "All right, I see how it is. Anyway, I don't think Hollie's here yet. I haven't seen her on the ice."

I sigh.

Cressie pulls her hairnet over her forehead. "Can I get you anything in the meantime?"

A slow smile spreads across my face. I pull out the nine quarters, stacking them neatly on the countertop.

"Nachos," I say, "extra cheese."

"You got it, girl."

While she's bustling behind the counter, I dream of the oozing yellow goo on a huge pile of deep-fried corn tortillas, salty on my tongue. Maybe it's not the *healthiest* snack, but today, I deserve it. I replay my encounter with Alex over and over in my head until I'm ready to burst with pride. The predator has become the prey.

Cressie unveils a magnificent pile of nachos.

"Careful," she says, "they're hot."

"Thanks, Cressie."

I carry my snack over to the locker room and crunch away like there's no tomorrow. I keep my eyes steady on the door until I hear footsteps coming closer. I jump up, nacho crumbs falling down my shirt.

"Hollie!" I shout as soon as I spot her blanket of blond curls.

I run up to her, ready to shake her shoulders and tell her my most spectacular news. But then I see her face. Hollie's cheeks are red and blotchy, her eyes puffy. She wipes away snot with the back of her hand.

"Hollie?" I skid to a stop. "Are you okay?"

Hollie's green eyes blink once, then twice, like she's just now registering who I am.

"Oh, hey, Maxine." She drops her skating bag on the ground. "Yeah, I'm okay."

My forehead crinkles. This is definitely not a portrait of someone who's "okay." The rings under her eyes are dark and shiny with freshly stained tears. I scan the doorway for her mom. She always stays for practice.

"Where'd your mom go?"

Hollie brushes past me, shaking off her coat and crumpling onto a bench. "Oh, she's . . . busy." She eyes my nachos. "Are these yours?" she asks. "Can I have some?"

"Of course."

She stuffs three entire chips into her mouth at once and licks the cheese off her fingertips.

"Mmmmm," she says, her eyes closed, "ah-mazinggggg."

She scoots over so I can sit beside her. I try to wait until she's done chewing before I say anything else. But she's just munching away, unstoppable. My eyebrows furrow.

"Are you sure you're okay?" I whisper.

She nods, offering a half-hearted smile.

"Don't worry," she says. Then, between bites: "You look like you had something to tell me?"

I sit up, squaring my shoulders. "Today, Porcupine Head was the literal worst."

Hollie groans, her eyes tinged with worry. "Oh no," she says.

"But then I did something awesome."

"What'd you do?"

"I gave it right back to him!"

Hollie flings her hands in the air, almost dropping the nachos.

"Oh my gosh, tell me everything."

"Well, I—"

"Maxine! Hollie!"

Hollie and I spin our heads around so quickly and so in tune, we could be synchronized skaters. Viktor and Judy are standing by the stairs, arms crossed. Judy's eyes narrow.

"Maxine Chen."

Oh man, not my full name again.

"Lace up. Both of you. You're three minutes late for warm-up."

I look at the clock. Darn it. Those seven and a half minutes somehow became eleven.

We scatter to the locker room before Viktor can shoot us one more evil death glare. When we're out of sight, Hollie takes my hand and squeezes.

"Later," she says, "I want to hear *everything*."

A Few Surprises

A new e-mail sings in my inbox: Eastern Sectionals are just eight days away! This year, they're in Cheshire, Massachusetts, a small town that sounds like it's straight out of a storybook. But when I step onto their rink, will the fairy tale be real?

Last night, Meghana and I practiced Choctaws until my feet ached, and then I spent an extra hour on double Axels with Judy, just to get them precise. Judy videoed each one on her phone, and then we played them back in slow motion to ensure that I didn't under-rotate or cut any corners. I can't afford to make mistakes this time. I've never been to sectionals before, but I can only imagine that it's way worse than regionals. Girls practically bungee-jumping into the air, layback spins so curved they could become acrobats when they're done with their figure skating careers.

DaMonique Sanders from Greensboro Skating Club is the one to beat. She is absolutely *astonishing*. I heard she beat the second-place finisher at her regionals by twenty-two points.

I shove my phone into my backpack, tucking it away between stacks of math homework and half-written English essays. I figure if I can't *look* at the e-mail, I'll stop thinking about it.

I focus on the face staring back at me in my locker mirror: oval forehead, thin cheeks, hair down for once, draping over my shoulders. My eyelids are smeared with shimmery purple. It's not nearly as good as Jennie's, but the Japanese girl on YouTube was going to have to do. It took me fifteen minutes just to figure out how to *not* make myself look like I was being punched in the face.

The bell rings. I swipe on cherry ChapStick and examine my reflection one last time. The sectionals e-mail still blares in my mind, a never-ending reminder that I have exactly eight days to prove that I can medal, that I'm worthy of the national championships. That one day, I might represent America, even if it is made up of all old guys. Even if—

"Maxine, hey."

Victoria stands in front of me, hugging her textbooks to her chest. Her doe eyes are wide, lashes curled so high they almost reach her eyebrows. Face-to-face for the first time in weeks, we study each other. Centuries seem to have passed since the last time we chatted at my locker.

"How are you?" she asks.

I shift in my sneakers. I wish I could tell her everything—the nightmares I've had, the laughter I hear in my sleep, the way her linked arm in Alex's makes me want to simultaneously vomit and hide in my locker for the rest of eternity so I don't have to ever see them again. I think about the stinging burns I could torch her with, just like Alex, just like he did to me. But as I look at her, I don't think I have the heart. She looks so small, so young.

"I'm good," I tell her.

She pulls at her skirt. So I guess she's no longer rocking the blueberry trend anymore. Violet from *Willy Wonka* never suited her anyway. She's much more of a Veruca Salt. Anyway, today she's dressed like a mini Prada model, with her black checkered skirt, kitten stockings, and distressed pleather boots. She rubs a hand along her jawline.

"I guess I'll see you in art," she says.

"Yeah," I reply, "see you."

Maybe I should feel upset, but I don't. My steps somehow feel lighter. Victoria isn't the first friend I've lost. In kindergarten, Sally Hughes played house with me every day for a week. And then the next Monday, she decided she didn't want to anymore. I remember crying for two hours straight, soaking Mom's blouse with my tears, my chest heaving so hard, my ribs felt sore. That night, Mom gave me this whole talk about how trees grow at different rates and every tree is different and maybe Sally and I were just sprouting on different timelines. I didn't understand her analogy at all. But I think that now I do. Victoria is a willow and I am an oak.

"Hey, Maxine?"

I turn. Victoria is halfway down the hall, her eyes searching mine.

"I just wanted to say that I like your makeup today." She smiles. "It looks great."

I let myself smile back. "Thanks."

I'm almost late to history, but I manage to slide into my seat just as the second bell ends. Mr. Warren is passing out permission sheets.

"It's late notice," he says, "but we just received approval from the Fort Ticonderoga Reenactment Society!"

The classroom suddenly fills with murmurs. Elisa cranes her neck toward me.

"My uncle was in one of their reenactments once," she says. "He got to play Ethan Allen."

Mr. Warren waves his hands up and down like he's conducting an orchestra instead of shushing a room of sixth graders.

"I know, I know, it's very exciting. Instead of school on Friday, we'll be heading to the site where America had their first victory against the British! Where they looted and captured the fort!" At every other word, he punches his arm in the air. He'd be great as a guide on one of those double-decker tour buses. He'd get tips for enthusiasm alone.

He runs his hand along the ends of his mustache. "That does mean, however, that I'll need these permission slips signed by a parent or guardian and returned to me tomorrow morning. Are we all clear?"

No one is paying attention to him. They are all too busy talking about how they're getting out of Friday's math test. Since the skits are over (Alex finally mumbled some nonsensical stuff about

John Laurens yesterday), Mr. Warren claps his hands, turns on the PowerPoint projector, and starts droning on about some other part of history I'm eventually going to have to memorize.

While I take notes, I notice Alex staring at me. Is he looking at my eye shadow? Is he going to say something about my face again? And what comeback will I have this time? But as soon as I make eye contact, he looks away, immediately turning to scribble in his notebook.

I smirk, just a little satisfied. Maxine: 2, Alex: 0.

Worried

By November, Lake Placid is cold and gray, at the start of a seemingly never-ending winter. Even we skaters have to bundle up in scarves as we flock to our icy home-within-a-home—our indoor winter that never ends.

Hollie doesn't realize this, though. She stalks into the rink with her windbreaker and Converse, a workbook tucked under her arm.

"Seventy degrees!" She pulls her phone from her pocket and waves it in my face. "It's seventy degrees in Virginia Beach right now."

I scrunch my nose. "That's practically summer."

Hollie flops down on the bench and pulls her hood over her eyes. "It's NORMAL weather. Now I can't even do homework outside."

She's still complaining when we get on the ice. During warm-ups, she keeps pausing to stare wistfully at the sliver of windows lining the rink, bare-limbed trees peeking in.

"Viktor's gonna yell at youuuuu," I whisper in a singsong voice.

Hollie pouts.

Lo and behold, 3.5 seconds later, Viktor emerges on the rink with his bleached undercut and bright red RUSSIA jacket (seriously, if he's trying to emulate a stoplight, it's working) and starts making wild hand movements at Hollie like he's trying to relay some secret code.

I roll my eyes and tug on her arm, pulling her toward her coach.

"At least you don't have to live in Russia!" I tease.

Hollie sticks out her tongue at me and dutifully skates over to Viktor.

Even if she won't stop complaining about the freezing Lake Placid air, I can tell she's happier today. Her eyes are clear and bright. But her sniffles and tearstained cheeks replay in my memory. We never talked about it. Not that we've had much time—with sectionals closing in, we've spent every spare moment on the ice, together but silent, the only sound our toe picks kicking up snow. I wish we could talk for a moment, for real, even though I'm not sure what I would say or how I could help.

Everyone on the rink has already started running their routines. I twizzle down the ice and admire my neat circles: one, two, three. Meghana really paid off.

Even under the stress of competition season, even with my lack of triple-double combinations, the slick ice feels like heaven. The night seems to drift on forever as I skate, and skate, and skate. Eventually, Judy says that she'll see me tomorrow and heads for home. I peer up at the giant digital clock hanging in the center of the rink. Thirty minutes left on the ice until Mom comes to pick me up. I look around. Only Hollie and I and a handful of other girls are still here. Even Viktor has left. I skate over to Hollie. She's finishing a scratch spin, her body turning so quickly, she's just a blurry shadow of freckles and hair. She slows to a stop.

"That was really beautiful," I admit, pointing at the etchings her blades have carved into the ice. "You barely moved an inch."

When spinning, you never want to travel too far. It's a sign of poor balance and not using your core. I touch my abs. While I've been doing crunches every day, I'm still not as steady as Hollie.

She blushes. "Thanks."

"Come on," I say, grabbing her hand, "let's do sit spins together."

Hollie laughs. She knows I'm mesmerized by the pair skaters; the fact that they know each other's minds and bodies so well that they can land jumps at the exact same time is legitimately incredible. I barely know what *my* body is going to do on the ice, much less someone else's.

We extend our legs and kneel to the ground, spinning beside each other, panting, and gulping the empty rink air.

"That was awesome!" I shout, wiping sweat off the nape of my neck.

"Yeah," Hollie replies, "we could give Sui and Han a run for their money."

She's grinning but her smile droops, her eyes glassy, like she's working really hard to show that she's happy, that she's okay.

I inch toward her. "Hollie," I say, trying to channel Mom's voice when she's coaxing me to tell her something, "what's wrong?"

"Nothing," she quickly replies.

I look at her. She looks back at me. Then down at the ground. She motions to the far side of the rink, and we drift to the boards.

"It's just," she says, "I've always gotten super nervous before competitions. And now, Mom's on my back more than ever and Viktor's, well, Viktor, and everything just feels like my normal nerves times ten." She gestures to the locker room. "And on top of that, I have loads of workbooks to do."

I rest a hand on her shoulder. "Yeah," I say, "that seems like a lot of pressure."

Hollie's eyes dart around the ice. She tugs on her pullover and leans in.

"Sometimes," she whispers, "I don't even know if I want to keep skating." Her bottom lip quivers when she speaks. "I mean, I love it, but I just don't know. The thought of being judged on the ice in front of all those people, all the time, well, it just . . . it feels exhausting. And it makes me kind of want to throw up." Hollie picks at her fingernails before glancing up at me, worry filling her eyes. "Sorry," she says, "I didn't mean to dump all that on you."

I freeze. Hollie? Not skating? But she's working on triple Lutz, double toe combinations. She was first at regionals. How could someone that good quit? I want to say all this to her, to shake her and tell her that girls would give anything to be in her skates, to be the best one in the arena. But then I look at the hollow lines of her cheeks, the way her eyes seem scared. Terrified, even.

"Don't apologize." I pat her back. "That's what friends are for."

Her lips turn up at the corners just a little. "Yeah."

"Have you thought about talking to your mom about how you feel?"

Hollie shrugs. "Not really. I don't think she'd understand."

"She might!"

I think about my own mom, pacing back and forth in the locker room, glancing at me in the rear-view mirror, a permanent crease nestled between her brows. How many times has she asked me if I need a break? But I guess all moms aren't like that.

"Just think about it," I say softly. "Maybe she'll surprise you."

"Maybe."

I fold my arms around Hollie. She smiles, hugging me back.

When we release, she peeks out at the ice. I can see the wheels turning in her brain.

"Double loops," she challenges me, "at the same time."

"You're on."

We skate into backward crossovers, our arms like compasses as we get ready to fly.

"One," she says.

"Two," I answer.

"Three!"

We take off.

The Field Trip

The Fort Ticonderoga Reenactment Society is located on acres of rolling grass, yellowed from the crisp air. A large stone wall encircles the fort, manned by old-fashioned artillery guns and a winding driveway. In the distance sits Lake Champlain and a rippling American flag.

Mr. Warren leads our class from the school bus to the visitors' entrance, where he makes us write down our names on stickers and press them to our shirts. Alex draws a tiny thumbs-down on the corner of his name tag. He's actually a pretty gifted artist. Too bad he's also so gifted at having a terrible personality.

Mr. Warren lays down the ground rules, repeating them three times in case we all collectively have amnesia or something. *1) Stay with the class. 2) Be polite to the actors. 3) Don't act stupid.* Mitchell is flipping his eyelids so that you can see the pink skin underneath. I think he's already broken rule number three.

We traipse to the first building where half a dozen dudes in ponytailed wigs are waiting for us. They're all in navy-blue coattails with brass buttons, standing straight in a row. Three of them are mannequins. A chandelier with candlelight bulbs flickers above the scene. A man in the center of the creepy group steps forward.

"Why hello, Mirror Lake middle schoolers! It's a pleasure to meet you. My name is Ethan Allen." His voice is stilted and overly cheery.

Elisa squints. "Well, that's definitely not my uncle."

Mr. Warren pushes us closer to fake Ethan Allen as the reenactor talks about the colonists, the

Green Mountain Boys, and their decision to raid and capture Fort Ticonderoga back in 1775.

My mind hovers on the word *Boys*. Are there any Green Mountain *Girls*?

Ethan Allen introduces the other two. I don't think Benedict Arnold or William Delaplace would be able to give me a straight answer—they're too busy going on and on about military tactics. They don't even get to the good stuff: the fact that Benedict was a traitor. I start drifting off, squeezing dirt under the soles of my sneakers and wondering if I close my eyes, I can transport myself to bed.

"Class?" Mr. Warren prods, eyeing the work sheets crumpled between our fingers. "Does anyone have any questions?"

"Yeah," Alex says, waving his hand high in the sky. "Boxers or briefs?"

A bunch of kids start giggling. Mr. Warren might murder Alex with his eyes.

"This is your first warning, Mr. Macreesy," he hisses.

Ethan Allen does not miss a beat. He smooths down his jacket and smiles at Alex, who is still fist-bumping his friends.

"I'd be happy to tell you a little bit more about fashion nowadays if you'd like. You see, these breeches..."

Eventually, we leave the Ethan Allen room and move to an artillery tent, where one man sits on a fake horse and tells us about Revolutionary War cavalry while another does a show-and-tell with a Pennsylvania Rifle, supposedly a favorite of the American soldiers. It's not *nearly* as cool as Mary Ludwig Hays's cannon. But I guess it'll have to do.

In another building, colonists wearing white puffy pants and little hats talk about sewing and shoemaking at Fort Ticonderoga. Later, in the old-time kitchen next door, we take turns churning butter and then spreading it onto salty crackers. It's smooth and delicious—way better than the mushy goop they serve at the cafeteria. Even Alex asks for seconds.

Maybe this field trip is kind of cool, after all. As I crunch through the grass, I breathe in the fresh air and the tangy taste of fall. The world feels peaceful. I'm holding a quill and ink that I bought at the gift shop during our lunch break. Elisa is chattering in my ear about who knows what, but I don't mind.

Finally, we reach the last building on our trip. Betsy Ross beckons us in, donning a muddy green dress with a lace collar and one of those classic white bonnets. She sits in a rocking chair, stitching something. As we get closer, I realize it's a version of the American flag, with thirteen five-pointed stars arranged in a circle in the left-hand corner.

"Betsy Ross *definitely* wasn't at Fort Ticonderoga," Elisa whispers.

Mr. Warren shushes her.

"I was just a simple seamstress," Betsy says, "until I became something far greater."

We lean in as she talks about the Union and the significance of the first flag, and what it meant for the United States they were trying to create. The reenactor's voice is lyrical and gentle, like a familiar lullaby.

"You know," Betsy says, "I wasn't the only woman fighting for the colonists. There were many who played pivotal roles in American history. Can anyone tell me some of their names?"

Elisa's hand shoots up. "Deborah Champion!"

"Ah yes," Betsy says, applauding, "she delivered urgent messages to George Washington in secret."

"Mary Ludwig Hays!" I shout, lifting my quill above my head. "She shot a cannon when her husband couldn't anymore."

"That's exactly right." Betsy Ross offers me a huge smile and I can't help but stand taller. "Do you remember what battle that was?"

I sure do.

"Yes, the Battle of Monmouth!" And for extra credit, I add: "1778."

"Well, well, well," Betsy Ross cheers, "don't we have a little historian in our midst."

"She's an excellent student," Mr. Warren says, winking at me.

I'm beaming. There is no chance on Earth that I'm going to be a historian, but it does feel good to excel at something other than skating. Wait 'til Mom and Dad hear. They'll be so pumped. Except then Mom will get excited and make me watch those boring documentaries with her. On second thought, maybe I won't tell them.

Betsy Ross continues while I do a little happy dance in my head. I'm still on cloud nine when I hear someone's loud breath inching closer and closer.

"I have a question," Alex says, but this time, not loud enough for Betsy Ross to hear, or even Mr. Warren. This one is just for me.

"Why are you even here?" he asks, his breath slimy and warm against my ear.

What? I think, my mind racing. *In this room? In this class? In this school? Where does he want me to go?*

"You don't belong."

His voice is louder now. Elisa and a few others around us can hear. Alex gestures to the crowd, and we both look at the pale, pale faces, and the hazel-eyed woman in her bonnet, and the blue-and-red-and-white flag sitting on her lap. I think my feet are glued to the floor. I try to recall comebacks or words, or anything, but I can't. I just can't. My brain is totally empty. And then it hits me.

Here, I realize. *He means here like America.*

And then he confirms it, his voice tight and ugly.

"You should just go back to where you came from, Maxine."

Now his words are loud, piercing, and everyone hears him. Betsy Ross has stopped talking. Mitchell is staring from under his mop of hair.

The world is silent but roaring in my head. I think pieces of me are falling apart. They're scattered everywhere, flying out of this room and into the afternoon air, somewhere far, somewhere terrible. Mr. Warren is swiftly shouldering through the students, barreling toward Alex.

Before I can even process my movements, I'm running into the open fields, as fast as I can go. My feet pummel through a flower garden as I sprint. I find myself heading toward the visitor center. I double over in the lobby, where a concerned woman with a badge that says FORT TICONDEROGA REENACT-MENT SOCIETY starts speaking rapidly into a phone. Time feels like it's going on forever and like it doesn't exist at all.

Finally, a hand touches my shoulder.

"Maxine?"

I turn. Mr. Warren is crouched behind me. I glance around, but none of the other kids are with him.

"I'm sorry," he says. "I'm so sorry."

I try to control myself, and act like the Maxine I desperately want to be—smart and calm and totally unafraid. Full of comebacks and witty responses.

But I am tired. Really, really tired.

So my head falls against Mr. Warren's shirt and my body heaves. At last, the tears come, and I let them flow down,

               down,

                    down.

The Truth

A woman is pacing outside Principal Perry's office. I know before she even enters the room—cushioning herself between Mr. Warren and me—that it's Mom, with her black bob and face filled with murderous rage.

"Mrs. Chen," Principal Perry says, smoothing her skirt as she stands, "thank you for coming in on such short notice."

It's only been three hours since our field trip was officially declared dead in the water. Whispers filled the bus as we rode back to school; I tried to ignore the sound of my name breathed through a game of Telephone. As soon as we arrived, Mr. Warren sent everyone to their next class and ushered me into the principal's office. Mom soon followed.

Now she straightens her shoulders, a classic Chen confidence booster, as if she's about to wage war against Principal Perry.

Mom is calm but her eyes are constantly darting to mine. I don't dare look back. Mine are still puffy from my last cry.

"Mr. Warren and I have already discussed the incident, but from what little Maxine has told us this afternoon, this apparently has been an ongoing issue," Principal Perry continues.

The three grown-ups turn to me. I sink into the leather chair. I know Alex is sitting outside with his own parents. I know the kids are still chattering in the halls. I know I'm front-page news for sixth-grade gossip. There's no turning back now.

So I tell them. I tell them everything. The self-portrait in art class, the eyelid tape, the math quiz, the library comments, the skit, and the field trip. I recall every smirk, every hushed insult—the words pour out of me, quiet and steady, in streams. When I'm finished, I exhale, staring at the floor as if my confession is a dark puddle seeping into the carpet. This is no comeback. This is surrender.

The office is thick with silence and squirms. Mom inhales, a slice of anger catching in her throat.

"Thank you for sharing, Maxine," Principal Perry says. "I'm sorry you experienced this, and I'm sorry that the administration could not step in sooner."

She pauses to scribble something on her notepad, her head shaking back and forth as she writes. "I want to reiterate that our school policy prohibits discrimination of any kind." She looks up at me. "There will be consequences for Alex's actions."

It's the first time today that anyone's said his name out loud.

Principal Perry tells Mom and me that she'll follow up with us shortly. Mom uses her telemarketer "I'm so grateful for your help" voice, her mouth in one of those canned smiles. I wait for her to switch into Scary Mom Mode, to wag her finger and tell everyone what's what.

But she doesn't say anything at all. Not in the office, or in the empty hallway, or in the car on the way back home. We drive past the rink where Hollie and the others are probably skating away, oblivious. I press my cheek against the sweaty passenger side window. Mom turns on some podcast about politics. She's still totally silent. I can't tell what she's thinking, and I can't look at her. For some reason, I feel more ashamed than ever.

When we finally arrive home, Dad's Buick is sitting in the garage. My head snaps toward Mom.

"Why is Dad home? It's not even three."

At last, Mom turns toward me.

"We wanted to have this conversation together, Maxine," she says.

We get out of the car.

Dad is sitting in the living room. "Hey, kiddo," he says, but his voice sounds strange, like it's lost in a long tunnel.

He pats the couch, motioning for us to sit beside him. I curl my feet under my thighs and wait for the lecture. I can just imagine it: *How come you never told us? How could you hide this for so long? Maxine, you know you can come to us for anything.*

But they don't say any of that. Instead, tears slide down Mom's cheeks and she quickly wipes them away with the back of her hand. I can't believe it. The last time Mom cried was when Nai Nai died seven years ago.

"Mom?" My voice is small and childish.

Dad rubs Mom's back and wraps an arm around me.

"Maxine," he says, "when your grandparents came to America, they were treated very poorly. They couldn't speak English. People were cruel."

Dad glances at Mom, who is sniffling but nodding at him to keep talking.

"When your mom and I got married and moved here, we thought that was all over. We were a little naive," he admits. "We didn't realize that pharmacy school was a bubble and that here, we'd be anomalies. We'd be treated differently. But we always believed that with each generation, people would be kinder, smarter. I mean, look at you, kid, you're so smart. Smarter than the two of us ever were."

"That's not true," I whisper.

Dad takes a deep breath. "We never wanted you to suffer. All we wanted was to shield you from hate. But clearly, we couldn't. I'm so sorry. I'm sorry that we failed."

I think he's crying now, too. My parents—pillars of strength—reduced to tears over a twelve-year-old boy. It makes me so angry.

"You didn't fail," I tell them, my voice louder than I anticipated. This is so stupid. Alex is so stupid. I want to punch him in the face. I want to throw him in the lake. I want to—

Mom sits up.

"Maxine," she says, "I want you to know that we are proud to be Chinese. Just as your grandparents were, and just as you should be, too. It's hard to feel this way when others want to tear you down. I think we all realize now that people like Alex are always going to exist." She pauses, like she wants to word everything exactly right. "They're always going to want to make you feel bad so they don't have to think about their own problems."

I don't say anything. All I can think about is a million Alex Macreesys forever and ever and ever. That sounds like a living nightmare.

Mom is no longer crying. She lifts my face in her palms.

"But there is one thing I know," she says, "that Alex certainly doesn't. That maybe you don't even know."

"What?" I whisper.

Mom smiles. "That no matter what, my daughter is a fighter. On and off the ice."

She kisses my forehead. *A fighter*, I repeat to myself, letting the words rest on my tongue.

Mom and Dad envelop me in a giant family hug. As they suffocate me with their embrace, I have to wonder if Mom's right. My comebacks didn't work, I sobbed on a class field trip, and I ended up in the principal's office even though I desperately tried to stay out of it. But at the end of the day, I guess I'm still here.

I lean into my parents. This time, I don't let them go.

Last Melody

Inhale, exhale.

It's our last day of off-ice training before sectionals. And although I still hate ballet, I do like this breathing exercise we're doing for the first few minutes of class. Winona has us standing at the barre, our backs arched, eyes closed, breathing to the beat of a ragtime melody.

Inhale.

Alex was only suspended for a day. And apparently he has to attend biweekly sessions with Ms. Callahan, our guidance counselor. I don't know if it'll change anything—or even if he can change—but Mom and Dad seem mildly satisfied. And no one says anything to me anymore; Mitchell hides behind his hair and the rest of the boys have scattered like flies. Elisa and I eat lunch together, sharing turkey sandwiches and pita chips. Thankfully she doesn't ever talk about the field trip—she's too busy rambling about black holes and whatever the heck gravity vacuums are.

Exhale.

Yesterday, Victoria waved to me in the hall. I don't think we're going to be friends again, but that's okay. I try to remember what Mom said about trees, and not just in relation to Victoria. There are ways in which I'm growing, too, inch by inch, reaching for the mountains.

"Sorry I'm late!"

Hollie comes running in, clumsily shoving her feet into ballet shoes. She stands behind me at the barre, wiping sweat off her hairline.

"Hey," I say.

I know she's smiling even though I can't see her face. "Hey," she replies.

The pianist spins up the octave into a lively carnival tune. Hollie sighs behind me.

"Man, now I want cotton candy."

"Mmm," I say, imagining the pink sugar melting against my tongue, "and kettle corn."

"Blech, kettle corn is gross."

"*You're* gross," I tease.

Hollie snorts. "At least I don't butt people when I plié."

For a moment, we stand in silence, and then I can't help but let out a giant laugh. Soon, we're both cracking up, bending over the barre, bellies bloated. The ballerinas are shooting glares so icy, they could turn us into giant Popsicles. Winona tiptoes over to Hollie and me like she's sneaking into a private sleepover.

"Girls," she hisses, "your glutes!"

I bite my lip to hold in the tremor of laughter still hanging in my throat.

"Sorry," Hollie says.

"Yeah, sorry," I echo.

We wait until Winona walks away before we whisper at the same time, giggling between words: *Girls, your glutes.*

When class is finally over, Hollie and I swing our backpacks over our shoulders and step out into the silent night air. The empty parking lot feels peaceful. And then, the headlights on her blue minivan blink once, twice. A woman waves from the car.

Hollie hesitates. I can see the worry scrawled onto her forehead in big, fat letters. The competition is only two days away, and the pressure is mounting—for Hollie most of all. She looks like she could choke on it.

"Hey," I say, poking her shoulder, "have you talked to your mom yet?"

Hollie thumbs the sleeve of her leotard.

"About what?"

"About how you feel," I tell her, "about skating."

Hollie's shoulders droop. "No, I haven't mentioned it," she says. "With sectionals coming up . . . it just feels like the wrong time."

I kick my feet against the gravel. Tiny stones fly into the air, like they're trying to make themselves heard. The sky seems to close in on us.

"Or it's the perfect time," I say.

We both stare into the darkness, the stars blanketing our heads. Suddenly, Hollie takes my hand, her palm cold in mine.

She squeezes. I squeeze back.

The Comeback

It's official—I have a dire medical problem: the ice has seeped into my veins. Seriously. After ballet yesterday, I managed to convince Mom and Dad to go back to the rink so I could run through my programs three more times. I've memorized the exact crunch of my blade after each jump landing—I know just how the wind feels on my shoulders as I zip around the rink.

This morning, with the sky still dark, I stretched my arms like a snow angel and pretended I was Michelle Kwan in her final pose at the 2003 World Championships. That was her fifth world championship win (seriously, she's a legend), so she didn't have to prove anything to anyone anymore. She just performed. At sectionals tomorrow, that's what I want to do. Enjoy the ice, and own every second of it. And hopefully medal. I *really* want to medal.

Now at school, as light begins to break through the clouds, I glance around the hallway. There's no one here—Mr. Warren and the others are still in the teachers' lounge. I got to school early today because we're going to pile into Dad's Buick and head to sectionals at noon. Mom says I might as well pick up my homework from my teachers first thing this morning. Instead, I do a three-turn hop in my sneakers and bounce across the tile, pulling my arms into a double flip.

And then . . . my foot hits someone's knee.

I spin around. Alex Macreesy is on the ground, grasping his leg in pain. His face is ashen and he's clutching a packet of papers that says *Growing and Understanding Each Other*. Of course—he's here for his guidance counselor sessions.

Time seems to move slowly. I can hear the

squeak of my sneakers as I tower above him. *Look who's a loser now.* The words want to spring out of my mouth. *Pathetic.* It would be so easy to say, so perfect. At the same time, I can't help but study Alex's tired eyes, his white knuckles clamped around the packet. A twinge of sadness punctures my anger.

I slowly bend down until we are face-to-face. Alex looks up at me. Reaching out my hand, I pull him to his feet. Now we are on equal footing. Alex's mouth parts and then closes and then opens again, but he says nothing. He doesn't move, either—he just stands there, papers to his chest.

I take a deep breath and remind myself that I, too, am standing. And for a moment, brief and warm, I don't feel alone.

Michelle Kwan is beside me, skates planted, sinewy arms firmly on her hips.

Mirai Nagasu is right behind, screaming triumphantly, her mouth open in a glorious roar.

Nathan Chen keeps close, with quads bundled

like grenades, tossing them forward until they cause an explosion.

Jennie is holding a mirror to my face, hers painted with a killer cat eye, bold and unafraid to be exactly who she is.

And then Mom and Dad emerge, hands on my shoulders, determined to lift me up—even when I'm ashamed, even when I'm scared.

My daughter is a fighter. Mom's voice reverberates in my ears.

There are a million Alex Macreesys out there. But I think I'll survive.

I brush past him, and my heroes follow.

I'm Maxine Chen. And this time, I don't think I need a comeback. I've got something far greater.

Singing Along

"Those summer . . . *NIIIIIIIIGHTS.*"

Dad is belting the entire soundtrack of *Grease* like he's auditioning for Broadway. Except—judging from his truly horrendous rendition from the driver's seat of our car—he's not going to make it through the first round of cuts. Mom stirs beside him, rubbing her eyes as she awakens from her rudely disrupted nap.

"Do we really have to do that now?" she grumbles.

"Yes," he says, "where's your spirit? Where's your *greased lightnin'*?"

Mom and I simultaneously roll our eyes. Did I mention that I have the dorkiest dad ever?

He's moved on to "Hopelessly Devoted to You," crooning as we cruise down the highway.

We've almost reached Cheshire, Massachusetts. Toasted red hills roll past us as we drive, parted only by farmland and a smattering of truly gigantic horses. We really are in fairy-tale land.

Tucked away in our trunk is all my skating gear—my dresses, and my fleece, five hundred bobby pins, and probably ten pounds of makeup. I could enter a beauty pageant with all this stuff. Spread out in the back seat, I dig my palms into my thighs, trying to keep the blood flowing. I'm pretty sure I'm not actually doing anything useful, but it keeps my mind busy.

Dad is now singing in a super high-pitched voice to re-create all of Sandy's parts. The more Mom glares at him, the louder he wails. I don't know if I'm going to win gold, but I definitely deserve an award for having the weirdest family ever.

My phone buzzes in the back pocket of my jeans. Hollie's name flickers onto my screen.

Hi! We are on our way. ☺ *U?*

I chuckle, thinking about how different our trips must be right now.

Yep, same! My dad is treating us to a *truly* great car ride concert . . .

Oh nooooo. Wicked?

Nope, even worse. Grease.

Yikes

Yupppppp

I watch the road blur past us. I wish Hollie was with us right now. We could play Twenty Questions or talk about books. Even though both of us barely have time to read, Hollie could spend hours reciting a novel she's memorized. It's her favorite thing to do when she's procrastinating. Ninjas and pirate queens dot her fantasy world and make us both feel less stressed about skating.

Hollie's name flashes once more on my screen.

Speaking of parents, I talked to Mom yesterday

I sit forward in my seat.

You did? How'd it go??!!

Idk, good I think? I said that I was feeling a lot of pressure and stuff and that competing was hard for me

I'm proud of you for saying that

Yeah. She didn't really get it at first but we talked for a loooooong time and I think she gets it a little more now.

That's good, right?

I think so? Anyway, we're gonna talk more about it after sectionals

Yay ☺ I'm happy 4 u

Thanks ☺ And thanks for being such a good friend

She keeps typing.

Even if you really suck at pliés

RUDE

Hehehehehe

I grin, sliding my phone into the cup holder.

Mom sighs loudly. "All right," she says, eyeing Dad, "if you're gonna sing, it's got to be something good."

She scrolls through his phone and pauses on a song, her fingers hovering as she offers a sly smile. She presses PLAY.

A familiar melody twinkles through the speakers. Teresa Teng's smooth voice envelops our car. Of course. Mom's favorite.

Dad sways along to the silvery tune. As we speed past wheat fields and deserted barns, Mom closes her eyes and starts singing along in Mandarin. The chorus builds.

This is the only Mandarin song I can sing. Mom used to lull me to sleep with it when I was a toddler, tucking me in and whispering words I didn't know but could feel on the tip of my tongue. It's been stuck in my memory ever since. I listen as my parents' voices swell with the music. And then I join in.

> *Wǒ de ài bú biàn,*
> *yuè liang dài biǎo wǒ de xīn.*
> My love will not change.
> The moon represents my heart.

Sectionals

Everyone is buzzing. You can feel it through the rink's padded blue walls and in the bleachers, where the scattered crowds of overeager parents and random old ladies from town enthusiastically wave every time you pass them during warm-up. I practice landing positions on the mat by the boards, pushing my arms out and pulling them in again and again. The first heat of intermediate ladies is warming up. Just a couple feet away, Mom and Dad are nervously stuffing their faces with nachos. Guess *that's* where my craving comes from.

I roll the balls of my feet against the floor. Outside this rink, it's a typical November day in

Massachusetts. To-do lists are written, phone calls are made, lunch is cooked. But in here, we'll remember today as one of the most important days of our lives. I just hope I can make it count.

The girls weave in mazes on the ice, careful not to run into one another. In the center of the arena, Hollie springs upward like a rocket. A triple Lutz, double toe. So she *is* actually attempting the combination at sectionals. Some skaters rely on their arms to get that extra bit of rotation. But Hollie doesn't do that; her powerful legs propel her straight up into three swift rotations in the air, followed by two and a half more, and a tight, checked, one-foot finish. Even DaMonique Sanders is casually eyeing the new competition from the sidelines.

A prickly voice announces that the warm-up is over: The short program has begun. The skate order is random, so Hollie happens to be skating third. Thankfully, I'm eleventh. Plenty of time to center my mind and stay calm. Or . . . to freak out. I mean, just look at the ten-foot podium perched behind the boards. It would be a nice nest for a giant. Instead, it's filled with stony-faced judges who have mastered the art of staring soullessly at the skaters below. I can already imagine them sizing me up, squinting at the monitor with robotic precision. My heart beats faster.

As if on cue, Judy surfaces from the locker room, beckoning me toward her.

"You shouldn't watch this," she warns. "It's not good for you."

She pulls on my arm, but I pull back. "I gotta see Hollie skate," I tell her, "and then I'll go in."

Judy raises an eyebrow.

"What?"

"Nothing," she says, but she's smirking. "Just thinking about how things have changed."

She lets go, and I return to the boards, eyes plastered to the glass.

The first two skaters are young and tentative. You can tell by their sluggish choreography and their two-footed jumps, the way their spins feel like they're going on forever, and not in a good way. It's hard to break in new ice. You have to really go for it, or you'll get lost in the shuffle.

Hollie is up next. She surveys the stands with mounting anxiety. Viktor offers her a stern nod and she moves into her opening pose. For a few seconds, she is simply a Spanish dancer, trotting down the ice to the sizzling tune of *Carmen*'s "Habanera." But then she powers through backward crossovers, and I know she's about to attempt her triple Lutz, double toe. You always try your most difficult element at the beginning of your program because it requires the most energy.

She toe picks on a back outside edge and takes off, spinning in the air once, twice, three times. And then—

She comes down with a crash.

Her hip hits the ice, a flurry of snow erupting in her wake. I stifle a gasp. Viktor is covering his eyes. But she recovers quickly—effortlessly landing a double flip and then a triple Salchow shortly after.

She shows no signs of stress as she offers the judges an air kiss with a cheeky wink. Her spins are elegant. I must admit—I get why she's Winona's favorite. And then, as soon as it has begun, her program is over.

When I have a bad skate, I stomp around like I'm trying to crush the ice into water. But Hollie just lowers her shoulders, cowering as she heads to the Kiss and Cry. Viktor squishes onto the bench beside her, rapidly shouting in a thick Russian accent. Hollie nods as if it's the only movement she's currently capable of making.

Only the skater and their coach are allowed in the Kiss and Cry, so I awkwardly pretend to stretch close by, tugging on my hamstring for the fourteenth time. Hollie sniffles. And then the mechanical loudspeaker lady is back, her measured voice betraying no emotion:

"The scores, please, for Hollie Westermann." The audience stills to a hushed silence. "She has earned a total score of 37.78 points and is currently in first place."

I watch Hollie's face fall in slow motion—her eyes drooping, her chin tucking into her neck. She may be in first place now, but there are fourteen skaters to go. Only four skaters move on to nationals. With that score, she's going to need a miracle to make it happen.

I rush after her as she slinks into the locker room, shielding her eyes with her skate guards. I swing open the door and find her curled in the corner.

"Hollie?" My voice is tiny and hollow, and feels like a million miles away.

Hollie looks up. Her cheeks are streaked with tears.

"Ugh," she says, wiping her face with the back of her hand, "this is so embarrassing."

"No it's not," I tell her. "It's just us."

For real—there's no one else in the locker room

since most girls go out to watch the competition or escape into the depths of the rink to find some peace and quiet.

"I fell," she says, her voice garbled with tears. She pulls her knees to her chest and dramatically throws down her head.

Geez, if I didn't know it, I'd think we swapped brains last night. And maybe we did, because the next thing that comes out of my mouth doesn't sound like me at all—it sounds like my mom.

"It's okay," I tell her, "it was just one jump. You have an entire free skate to go."

Hollie groans even louder as I come sit next to her, squeezing into the corner.

"I have so many points to make up," she says. For the first time, I can hear her worry press against her throat like a monster. Fat water droplets now fall down her shirt.

"Yeah," I admit, "you do. But you're one of the only girls attempting triple combinations, and you've landed them consistently at practice. The free skate can change everything."

As I'm dishing out advice, I try to believe what I'm saying. *My daughter is a fighter*, Mom said. And I know Hollie is, too.

Right now, she needs to know more than I do. So I make the ultimate best friend sacrifice, the true seal of devotion. I walk across the room, rummage through my skate bag, and emerge with the one thing I wanted all for myself but am offering to Hollie instead: a gooey, delicious chocolate fudge brownie. It's neatly wrapped in cellophane, still warm.

Hollie's face lights up as I place the brownie in her open hands.

"Where'd you get this?" she asks, as if brownies don't exist outside Lake Placid.

"The bakery next door," I tell her. "It's right next to the rink."

She meticulously unwraps the cellophane and

takes a large bite, her eyes closed like she's being transported to some chocolate utopia.

We sit in silence as she chews, her tear stains drying against her skin.

And then, with wide-open eyes, she looks right at me. Her voice is hushed but sure.

"This is the best brownie I've ever had," she proclaims. "Thank you."

I grin, rolling my eyes as she takes another big bite.

Let's Do This

I'm staring at my name on the laptop screen, right below five others, bold letters on a white background. No matter how many times I refresh the page, the short program results are not going to change. I'm in sixth place. Hollie trails close behind, in seventh. I didn't make any major errors—my double Axel and triple toe were fine and my step sequence was sharp. But I guess my double Lutz, double toe was kind of wonky, and I didn't get full credit on my Biellman. This is not some small-town competition—this is Eastern Sectionals. The field is deep.

Masha Stepanov is now competing for the

United States because making the nationals team in Russia was too difficult. She's doing Tanos (a move made famous by figure skater Brian Boitano) with her arm looped over her head; these make her jumps twice as difficult and give her extra points. And you know how Jesus walked on water? Well, Lucy Yeh might just give him a run for his money. She can basically levitate. Seriously. Her skating is so light and graceful that I secretly think she's an angel sent from heaven simply to spin around in skates. And then, of course, there's DaMonique Sanders. The powerhouse. She may also sneak a triple combination in her free skate—I wouldn't be surprised.

Only four girls go to nationals. I'm so close I could stretch my arm and graze the podium. All I have to do is touch it. Or just as easily, my grasp could slip and my season could stop here. End of the road.

Mom comes up behind me and hugs my shoulders, encrusted in silver beading and black velvet for my free program. She gently closes her computer and unfolds her hand, her palm brimming with with bobby pins. We stand together at the desk in our hotel room, shadows of each other as she pins my bun.

"Focus on yourself," she says. "None of those other girls matter."

I nod, although bees are still zooming through my insides.

Mom sticks so many pins in my hair that my bun wouldn't move if an earthquake hit it. She smooths down flyaways with the tips of her fingers.

"Skate your best. That's all anyone can ask of you," she tells me, kissing the top of my head.

"Okay," I say, "I will."

I turn around and Mom reaches out her hand to touch my chin. She pauses, her fingers hovering before my face.

"Your makeup," she says, "it looks lovely."

So she noticed! I've been practicing for weeks. I've got a long way to go until I'm as skilled as

Jennie, but I am relatively competent at sweeping bronze eye shadow on my lids and flicking liquid eyeliner above my lash line. When I examined my handiwork in the mirror this morning, my eyes shined like bright, brown almonds. They looked pretty.

Mom shakes her head. "Maybe you should be giving *me* makeup tips." She laughs.

My grin feels wider than my face.

An hour later, Hollie and I are doing squats by the boards, like that's going to suddenly turn us into world-class champions. We skate one after the other: our shots at the podium are just moments away. The crowd is sparse, but energized. A few parents carry giant, handmade signs with their children's names on them in fat marker and poster paint. Hollie's mom cranes her neck from the stands, but Hollie isn't looking at her. As her name is called for the free skate, she stares straight ahead, focused on the ice.

"You okay?" I ask.

Hollie rolls her shoulders. "Let's do this," she says.

I smile. I don't think I've ever seen her more determined. That chocolate must be working wonders.

The crowd hushes and Hollie begins her routine, the echo of Celine Dion's sugary voice enveloping the rink. Her blades scratch the ice. I find myself holding my breath as she extends her leg, flying backward at an impossibly fast rate. And then she's in the air. Triple Lutz. Double loop. Double toe. My jaw drops. A three-jump combination at the intermediate level—impossible.

I expect jealousy to fill my veins, but strangely, I don't feel that at all.

Instead, I find myself clapping as my best friend delivers a near-perfect routine.

The Final Skate

"Our next skater is Maxine Chen, representing Lake Placid Skating Club."

Picture this: You're standing in the center of the world. You can see only your reflection, delicate and beautiful below your feet. The air feels cool on your tongue. You are rooted. You are steady. And then, with a rush of piano keys, the music begins.

My arms are flower petals, blooming open as I dance across the ice, making use of all those Choctaws Meghana ingrained in my brain. I swerve into backward crossovers, hands turning like windmills to accelerate. Three-turning so I'm facing forward, I charge for the boards. You have to just go for it, I tell myself, don't hesitate. *You got this*, Mirai Nagasu whispers. Michelle Kwan nods from the other side.

The earth blurs. And then—I jump. Two and a half double Axel rotations sprung high in the sky. I'm moving faster than I can think. Finally, everything slows, and my blade hits the ground, perfectly angled on the ice. I can't see her, but I know Judy is yelling my name. Dad is tracking me through his dinosaur-age video camera and is zooming in way too close.

I land my triple toe without even thinking. Soon enough, I'm twisting into a layback spin, watching the ceiling coil. The Gershwin melody embraces my skin. There's something so magical about turning faster than seemingly humanly possible. For a moment, the rink, the scattered audience, and the judges melt away. No one else exists. I find myself smiling. I could stay here forever.

I can't, though, of course. And before I know it, I'm striking my final pose. Mom and Dad rise to their feet in the stands. Judy whoops from the boards, a loud "Yes!" escaping her lips. Hollie jumps up and down, her hair flying into her face. And I, gasping for air, take a bow.

I don't know what's going to happen next. I don't know who will win. But for this singular moment, I'm happy with the rush of adrenaline racing through my veins. I'm happy with the way the music swallows me whole.

The Beginning and the End

It's the best routine I've ever completed. The monitor confirms it with a small red box next to my score reading SB—Season's Best. Judy shakes my shoulders, and Hollie rushes toward me when I emerge from the Kiss and Cry. But then DaMonique Sanders steps into the arena, and I know it's over. The scoreboard flashes the current standings:

MASHA STEPANOV—119.63

HOLLIE WESTERMANN—115.21

LUCY YEH—110.07

MAXINE CHEN—108.90

If DaMonique places anywhere above me, then the podium slips away.

On the ice, she lifts her chin, arms raised in a diamond above her head, showcasing her sheer sleeves and bejeweled burgundy dress. She looks like a queen. Probably because she's about to be crowned. I'm sure the second the *Romeo and Juliet* selection begins. I'm sure when she spins into an effortless layback. I'm sure when she completes a successful triple flip, double toe. And I'm sure when she finishes her error-free program, toe pick in the ice, triumphant.

My body feels numb. I won't taste the medal. My photo won't be featured in some fancy East Coast newspaper. My costumes will go back in my closet, wrapped in plastic, saved for the next city competition or recital. We'll drive back to New York, and I'll just be me, Maxine. The skater. But not the girl going to nationals. The announcer confirms DaMonique's astronomic final score, 126.05, and she soars into first place.

On the bench by the boards, Judy wraps a puffy sleeve around my back.

"Maxine Chen," she says.

My pulse quickens at my full name, but when I look up, she's smiling. She tucks a loose strand of hair behind my ear.

"You just skated your personal best," she says. Her voice is heavy with pride.

She's right, I know. I fold my head into the crook of her neck. Mom and Dad jog down the bleachers, their gloved hands outstretched to reach mine.

I swallow the lump tugging at my throat. So I'm not going to nationals just yet. But it's okay. I'm going to be okay. I feel both sweet and strange.

Lifting my head from her shoulder, I look back at Judy, staring right at her with wide, unflinching eyes. If I've learned anything from sectionals, it's that I've got so much to learn and so much more to grow.

A burst of excitement cracks through my disappointment.

Today, I skated my season's best. *And* my personal best.

This is just the beginning.

Home

It's my favorite part of every competition. The short period of time right after it wraps up, before the next batch of junior ladies or senior men are about to make new scratches on the ice. The rink is still. You can no longer hear the booming loudspeaker or the crowd stomping their feet, or a skater's gasp as she receives her score. Now there's a clean slate.

Usually, I go out here by myself to collect my thoughts. But this time, I have a slightly different plan.

"Are you sure we should be doing this?" Hollie whispers as we tiptoe down the hallway and into the empty arena. Her eyes dart left and right like Viktor's going to pop out from underneath the bleachers.

"It's fine," I assure her. "Just for a couple of minutes."

I unzip my jacket pocket and take out my phone, placing it on the ridge of the boards.

"Besides," I say, a mischievous glint in my eye, "we deserve to celebrate."

What I don't say is that this could be the last time we get to do this at all. Since I finished in fifth place, I'm the first alternate for nationals. I won't go to San Jose. Instead, I'll cheer on Hollie from home as she skates circles around the other competitors. And when she returns, I'm not sure if she will even *have* any more medal ceremonies. Yesterday, Hollie admitted that this might be her final year competing. She's going to keep talking about it with her mom, but the pressure of performing day in and day out may be too much for her. I can understand that.

Hollie eyes my phone with great suspicion.

"Ready?" I say.

"Definitely not," she replies, but a small smile creeps onto her lips.

I press PLAY. "No Diggity" blares from the tiny speaker. We wiggle onto the ice. I do the sprinkler because that's Dad's go-to dance move, and Hollie pretends to swim underwater, plugging her nose and shimmying down to her knees. We try to rap the first part of the song, but fail miserably—skating and singing at the same time is really difficult. I make a show of doing a very poor butt plié. Hollie laughs so hard, tears wet the rims of her eyes. We dance all the way through two choruses, twirling down the ice until the rink door bangs open and Mom comes barreling down the hallway.

Hollie freezes in place, but I keep dancing.

"Did Maxine talk you into this?"

"Yes," we say simultaneously. There's no point in denying it now.

"Why am I not surprised?" She waves us off the rink. "Come on."

Hollie leaves first, chattering about how sorry she is to Mom, who is rolling her eyes and trying not to smile. But I take a moment to peek back at the ice, still smooth and glossy, still waiting for me to make my mark. I decide that I will, even if it's messy, even if it takes time. Three years may not be enough and that's okay. I've got a village to keep me going, to remind me that no matter what:

This is where I belong.

Author's Note

I first started skating after watching *Ice Princess* and immediately begged my parents to give me lessons. I remember giggling with my friends on the rink, convinced that one day we were going to be on television. I was a pretty terrible skater, though, so that was never a real possibility. What happened instead was so much greater—this book. While I did my absolute best to convey the reality of figure skating today, I did take a couple of artistic liberties. For example, as of 2020, intermediate skaters like Hollie and Maxine would no longer attend nationals should they qualify. Instead, the top skaters are named to the National High Performance Development Team and participate in a training camp. For American skaters to remain competitive, the rules and regulations must be adjusted all the time to reflect developments in the sport. In competitions across the globe, skaters are pushing themselves to new heights and achieving incredible feats. It's as exciting as it is groundbreaking. In this story, I'm honored to celebrate the history of figure skating and the journey of young, vibrant skaters like Maxine now and to come.

Acknowledgments

I wish I could hand out gold medals to each and every person who helped make this dream a reality.

Wes Adams, thank you for encouraging me to tell this story; your patience, keen eye, and abundant wisdom have made me the writer I am today. Melissa Warten, a true queen, thank you for championing Maxine, and for always answering my three hundred questions. Cassie Gonzales, you are an unparalleled designer and friend. I am shouting your name from the rooftops. My publicist extraordinaire, Madison Furr, thank you for sending Maxine out to the best events. Thank you, Taylor Pitts, Celeste Cass, Jessica White, Diane Joao, and Kiffin Steurer for your rigor and precision. Finally, to my entire FSG and MCPG family, but especially Joy Peskin, Grace Kendall, Janine O'Malley, and Trisha de Guzman, you are seriously rockstars. I am one lucky girl.

Dung Ho, your art is stunning. Thank you for bringing *The Comeback* to life. And a million thanks to Alice Min for being the wisest pseudo–skating coach, friend, and reader a writer could ask for.

To my incredible agent, Marietta Zacker, thank you for cheering on Maxine from the stands; I'm so lucky to have you on my team.

Sarah and Norah at The Bookstore Plus, thank you for your enthusiasm and excellent notes. The best Lake Placid bookstore of all time!

To my Instagram skaters: Masha, Grace, and Caroline, thank you for offering your insight into the current competitive skating world. Good luck out there—as Maxine would say: *You got this*.

Thank you to my Barnard babes, my Albany crew, and Emily Pratt for listening to me complain about writing, talk forever about skating, and then actually finish a book! I love you all so, so much.

Laura Schreiber and Tanusri Prasanna, thank you for your advice and constant faith in me. And Mini-Mouse, thank you for letting me use your name.

To all the teachers and librarians who cheered me on along the way: Sara LePore, Kimberly Murray, Hope Dils, Siobhan Matrose, Timea Szell, Jenny Boylan, and Mary Gordon—thank you for your inspiration, intelligence, and craft.

Thank you to the Asian American icons who paved the path, who were bold and brave in an unjust world.

Lastly, I would be nothing without my family. Grandma, thank you for loving and supporting me unconditionally. Mom and Diana, thank you for being my #1 fans, the Olympians of my heart. You are in everything I do, and in everything I am.

And Dad, thank you, always. I love you, I miss you, and I hope I've made you proud.

GOFISH

QUESTIONS FOR THE AUTHOR

E. L. SHEN

When did you realize you wanted to be a writer?
As soon as I could read! In first grade, I wrote these tiny stories, hole-punched them, and proudly gave them to my teacher. He humored me by putting them in the reading bins for the other children in my class to peruse. I didn't put my name on them, so my classmates would unknowingly pick up my "books" and flip through them—I felt like a celebrity in disguise! From then on, I learned how to hone my craft through writing workshops, college courses, and even a job in publishing. ;)

What challenges do you face in the writing process, and how do you overcome them?
Fear of starting. Worrying that all my words are wrong. Fear of ending! There's a lot of vulnerability that comes with writing. It's like putting little parts of your soul on paper and then silently watching people react. But I try to remember that there's a beauty in that too; strangers can suddenly relate to feelings you were never able to articulate aloud, and put new meaning into your

text. That's what keeps me writing even during the worst bouts of writer's block.

What was the inspiration for this book?

I took figure skating lessons for several years and developed a love for the sport. I was particularly obsessed with it during the 2018 Olympics. Around the same time, I had a conversation with my friends about a comeback list I had created when I was in middle school—anytime I was bullied, I wrote down the insults and my fake responses so I would be "prepared" for next time. One of my friends offhandedly mentioned that this would be an amazing book idea. So when I sat down to write Maxine's story, I realized that my love for skating and my middle school antics would marry into a perfect middle-grade. Maxine's determination and spunky personality flew off the page, and the rest is history.

In what ways does the racism experienced by Maxine at her school reflect the racism you experienced as a young person?

While Maxine's exact experiences with racism were not directly mine, they certainly mirrored the types of bullying I received in elementary and middle school. At the time, I couldn't even qualify them as "racist" because I didn't know what that meant. Like Maxine, I was too afraid and too proud to tell my parents. There's a great sense of shame that comes with bullying, and it's hard to break out of. There are also no easy solutions to micro- and macro-aggressions, but I hope that readers come away realizing that they always have teachers, friends, and loved ones they can turn to when they need help.

The Comeback was published in 2021, a year when there was a marked increase in racist acts against the AAPI community in the United States. Can you share some of your feelings about this?
Hate crimes against the AAPI community have existed for as long as Asian Americans and Pacific Islanders have been in America. I was horrified to watch them rise even more. Throughout the worst of the hate crimes—which are still ongoing—I thought a lot about how I coped when I experienced racism as a child. For me, one book offered me a great deal of comfort. It was _Good Enough_ by Paula Yoo. When I discovered it, I literally felt like I had found a best friend. I had never read a book about an Asian American protagonist before, much less a girl like me who loved music, had big dreams, and seemed invisible to her classmates. I could recite whole chapters from that book now, I think.

Often, you feel a deep sense of loneliness and help- lessness when reading about and watching videos of violence against the AAPI community. But as a child, it was helpful for me to remember that Patti in _Good Enough_ experienced the same thing. And if she could end up okay, so could I.

Books are not going to change racism. They are not going to stop people from hurting the AAPI community. But they can offer a light to those who need it desperately. They can be lifelines. I hope that *The Comeback* can be a semblance of that for young readers today.

Did you give Maxine any aspects of your own personality?
Definitely! Maxine's spunk and brazenness are based on my own. She's also stubborn and vulnerable, flaws I certainly see in myself.

In what ways are you and she different?
While I do skate, I'm not nearly as good as Maxine (although I aspire to one day get closer to her skill level!). And she is even more determined than I am—her aspirations for the Olympics are very real; my childhood skating dreams were extremely flimsy and literally based on one watch of the *Ice Princess* movie.

How did you celebrate publishing your first book?
By celebrating with my editor, family, and friends and eating tons of delicious chocolate cake. :)

If you could live in any fictional world, what would it be?
Narnia. Do you know how many times I walked into closets, closed my eyes, backed into some coats, and hoped I'd end up meeting Mr. Tumnus?